THESE ISLANDS HERE

SHORT STORIES OF THE SOUTH PACIFIC

BRONWYN ELSMORE

The stories included in this collection are set mainly in Aotearoa-New Zealand, though some are of, or include mention of, other islands of Polynesia.

They are fictional tales based on events and conditions of the recent (since c. 1800) history of Aotearoa-New Zealand and its neighbours. Together they present the varied facets of living in these islands situated in the South Pacific – pleasure, pain, calamity, comedy, fun, misfortune, loss, triumph – indeed, as in any part of the world, of being human.

Most have been published previously. Eleven have appeared in magazines including *NZ Listener, Takahe, Eve, Thursday*, and some newspapers; four have been included in anthologies; and seven broadcast by Radio New Zealand. Five have won short story competitions, and others have been placed or gained commendations.

Contents

1800s

The 1800s were times of much social adjustment in Aotearoa-New Zealand. Due to a wish to protect the country's first-nation people, Māori *or* tangata whenua, *from exploitation through the lawlessness of some Europeans, and to avoid the country's annexation by the French, the Declaration of Independence of New Zealand was proclaimed in 1835, and in 1840 the British government entered into a treaty with Māori.*

The establishment of a colony brought about increasing settlement from Europe, and within a short period Māori lost their position of sole permanent inhabitants, being quickly outnumbered by settlers. Their traditional customs and beliefs underwent much change, and dissatisfaction with dealings over land led to localised battles between Māori and British troops.

The lives of the new settlers were also greatly challenged as they sought to adapt to different conditions so far from family and all that was familiar. They came from all parts of the British Isles, Germany, France, Portugal, Netherlands, Denmark, USA, Canada, many coming via Australia.

Though the society created reflected the values and customs of Europe, the new land also provided a certain freedom from restrictions that many of the immigrants sought to escape. One notable example is that in 1893, with the passing of the electoral bill giving the vote to women, New Zealand became the first nation to allow its adult citizens universal suffrage.

OUTCAST

There could be no more delaying. Now she would have to go. For more than three days she had lingered, waiting as long as possible in the hope she could stay with the ones she loved.

But now the final pronouncement was made. They had come to her, looked, and their reddened eyes had accepted the inevitable. The tears and the anguish diminished, even in those closest to her, and the call was raised for her dismissal. Despite their sorrow there would be anger if she would not go willingly, for now fear was there, becoming more evident in the voices of the people as the calls that she be gone increased. It had to be. She knew that as well as they did.

When the cries reached a crescendo she rose from her position, passed between those surrounding her, and crossed the courtyard to the gate. They let her go without a sign that she had made her move, but as she passed between the standing posts her sister let out a loud wail. Looking back, she saw the women still grouped on the veranda, sitting hunched over what she knew was her lifeless body, rocking themselves back backward and forward, backward and forward. And now several of the men – her sons, her nephews – were climbing the hill behind the house grasping their digging sticks.

For some time, she stayed just outside the compound, watching as the rest of the company mounted the slope bearing their load between them, and carried out the rites. Before she stirred again they had returned, washed, and were again gathered at the central place.

They were her people. Sister, two brothers, aunts, uncles, cousins – all were there. And her children – they too were present, among the others.

Steam rose from the umu as the leafy coverings were removed from the earthen cooking pit, and the smell of hot food wafted in the air. She could see the family sitting and eating with the others, picking up kūmara, aruhe, and fish. For some it was the first food they had eaten since she had left them, and the beginning of the rites, nearly four days ago.

So many times in the past she had joined them in such occasions. For the last dozen years it had been she who had led the group. When it was Taranga's turn to be cast out, as with Rewa's, Hata's, Mihi's, and a score more, hers had been the voice that led the ritual cry. Go, go. Leave this place. No matter how many times there had been, over a lifetime of years, so many of which she had been at the forefront of the action, now it was her turn to look on from the outside. Separated from her family. Apart from her people. Removed from her home, her place to stand.

As it was for the others before her, there could be no return. No more could she join the ones who were left in the place that had been hers. After they had eaten would come the rites of cleansing. There would be chanting, wailing, as they trampled the ground. Rituals with water – sprinkling, washing – as they worked to cleanse the house, her home, of her presence. To make it safe from the pollution that had come from her passing into the world beyond. She knew how it would be in the future if they saw any sign of her being in attendance. There could never be understanding, mercy – she had joined the ranks of the unwelcome. They had uttered the words that cast her out.

So she must go. Giving the scene one last look, she set out.

The path away from the village sloped downward. She skirted the cultivated area where little grew at the moment. Part of the earth was turned over. The digging had begun for the spring planting, but then abandoned temporarily for the rites. When it started again tomorrow all would be as it was before. Except that she would not be a part of it.

At the base of the hill she turned north and travelled the familiar path, not stopping as she neared the kāinga of people she had known throughout her lifetime, relatives, her natal kin. They would not be there, she knew. Hadn't they been with the gathering at her own village – come to lend their voices to the others, insisting that she be sent out? Instead, she moved on, covering the ground at a pace that increased with each step that took her further from the home she had known for so many decades.

When she came to the place where the great river branched she took the path that went straight on. To the west wound the way to a village she had visited many times before. But this was not an occasion for calling, for sitting and talking, for sharing in the kai and the work. No food would be offered to her any more. Those times were past, over, not to return, and neither could she.

The way ahead led through a section of dense bush. Only once had she been this far before, and that was when she was a young woman, a long time ago. But her path was clear and she travelled on, not stopping to rest. She met no one else on the journey, though at times she sensed the presence of someone a distance ahead of her on the path. Then she hurried to catch up but could see no other form in the dim light.

After some time, she passed from under the thick canopy and

continued her hurried progress, this time along a shore, with long stretches of sand underfoot and to her left. Still she was not tired, and moved fast along the track. It was a long time since she had felt such energy, such freedom of movement, being able to move her limbs without stiffness. Now that she had reconciled herself to the break, had left the life she had known so far behind, she felt the exhilaration of release.

With the feel of the sun behind her, and the heat of the day-warmed sand encouraging rather than slowing her progress, she continued to move onward. It seemed her pace quickened with each step she took. Even though she had never been so far north before, had not travelled in this part of the country, she had heard the stories of the journey she must make, and knew she must go on even further before she could stop. Before she could finally find rest.

As well as the huge dunes on her left, now she could sense there was sea away to her right also. Soon the salt tang hung around her on all sides. The vegetation around her grew sparser and more stunted, then there was little left but scattered clumps of dry tussock – so different from the lush vegetation of the land around her own kāinga. It was no wonder there was no evidence of habitation, no sign of a living soul.

For a while the path kept climbing, but she reached a point where she stood on a small plateau and could see ahead. The path ran downward in front of her, just a short way to the ocean. On the horizon a group of islands showed dimly in the gathering dusk. Wheeling above, the gulls screamed over the crash of the waves that rushed onto the rocky shore. So this was it – the place to which she had been sent, exiled, banished. The place to which she herself had sent so many others before her.

There was no reluctance in her now. All the unwillingness

of the days before as she had resisted making the journey had gone. Instead, a new longing overtook her. Despite the years that had slowed her steps more and more in recent times, she ran down the slope and clambered over the rocky ridge above the sea. Waves beat at the low cliff on each side, and looking down she could see the large mass of seaweed writhing under the surface – a living door to the world below.

There was the single pohutukawa below her, just as she knew it would be though she had never been this way before. Its branches overhung the small cliff, reaching toward the water, its thick roots on the downward side running down the crumbly drop, pointing the way.

Easily now she slipped down to the tree below her, following the exposed root for the last part of her journey. Letting it lead her downward, she soul-slid down till the ocean surrounded her.

Back at the kāinga the people would have finished their meal. The karakia and the sprinkling of water would be over, the visitors saying their farewells and preparing to travel homeward.

"Go to your ancestors! Go to Hawaiki!" they had commanded her. "Hinenuitepō has come for you, so you must go."

"E Hine..." The cry came not from her mouth but from her soul. "E nga tūpuna..." The hand that formed the last link relaxed, and the root of the pohutukawa slipped through her fingers as the mass of kelp closed over her head.

DEADWOOD, LIVEWOOD

Lydia could hear the dull rhythmic sound of the plane working the wood.

Edward was right across the other side of the yard, sitting just where he had on the other occasions – on the seat he'd made on top of the stump of the old karaka tree. The memory of that tree still made her shudder. When she remembered the times she had spread a rug under its branches and let the little ones crawl about. Unknowing. Until the day they found Rover convulsing, unable to walk. Wikitoria had diagnosed the cause, hefted the old dog into her arms and carried him home with her.

"My aunty, she knows what to do."

By the time she returned, three days later, Rover trotting along behind, the tree was down; Edward had stacked the split wood against the back wall of the house, ready for winter, and the area around the stump had been scoured for any remaining bright orange berries.

The piece of timber Edward was shaping was braced between his left thigh and the outstretched right foot. If she turned her head, Lydia could see him bending and straightening as he worked the wood.

The deadwood.

It was just like the other times when he'd sat there, bent on the same task. But this time there were no flowers on the pohutukawa trees she could see on the rise in the distance. On the first occasion she'd stood and gazed at the scarlet-laden branches for most of the day it seemed. Yet not at them. Through them, past them, not really seeing anything for the blurring tears in her eyes.

The next time was barely a year after the first, and she remembered that only the first traces of colour were showing. A week later when the trees were aflame and she stood staring at the riot of scarlet again, it was a double ache she felt.

The following year the trees bloomed early – portent of a long hot summer, she was assured by Wikitoria. But the sight had put a fearful dread in her heart till the red blooms had dropped. Twice more after that the trees flowered without Edward sitting there at his task, and with the passing of that particular time in those years she breathed more easily.

But now he was there once more. A different season this time, but again he sat to work the deadwood. Now she knew it could happen anytime, and now the fear would never be gone fully.

The sound paused for a while as her husband turned the timber, then he began to work the other side. It would go on for hours, she knew. He could have chosen a smaller piece so there would have been less to work, but she said nothing. For a good part of the day he'd sit there, planing off layer after layer until just a narrow board was left of the original beam – and all around where he sat would be a mass of shavings. That was his therapy, she understood.

Tomorrow he'd saw the slim plank into two parts and fix the shorter one across the longer, taking great pains over the fitting of one into the other. Then it would be painted white before he brought it to her to see. And they would talk about the words to be painted on the crosspiece.

Not that there was much need to discuss it. Each was simple

and similar. 'Emily Louise Halbert, 1851-1855. Suffer the little children to come unto Me'. Then 'Sarah Elizabeth Halbert, 1853-1856' with the same text.

This time, though, the words might be different. Those didn't seem quite so suited to young Leonard. Perhaps a simple 'called to be with the Lord'? Yes, that would do – 'Leonard Edward Halbert, 1848-1859. Called to be with the Lord'.

Emily and Sarah – they had really suffered. The fever, the growing delirium passing into great spasms, and then the agonizing gasping for breath before the end. And she almost helpless to help except for keeping the little bodies cooled with wet towels.

When Emily was at her worst Wikitoria told her of a healer, a tohunga at Maketu, and she was ready to send for him. Edward on his own she might have persuaded to agree, but the vicar who visited, prayed and shook his head, condemning the idea as a heathenish practice, calling it "witchcraft of satanic derivation". With that hope gone, Wikitoria tried to soothe her by saying that her priest may not have been able to help anyway. His remedies were against the mate Māori – the mate Pākehā, ah that was another thing. Wikitoria continued to visit the house after Emily went, but she didn't attend Sunday service with them again. Then it was the turn of little Sarah, who had always been the Māori woman's favourite. After that, Wikitoria took frequent trips away from the township, never speaking of her new beliefs, but it seemed that the gap between them widened.

Lydia turned her head to look across the yard. Still her husband continued to work – his arms and shoulders bending and straightening, bending and straightening as he worked the deadwood. A wave of revulsion and pity passed over her.

Revulsion for the deadwood itself, pity for the man who had to fashion it. She started to move toward him, to stand behind him as he worked, her hand on his shoulder. But another movement stopped her after a single step – a movement below her bodice, and the strongest she had felt yet. Slipping her hand beneath her apron she placed it on her belly where the fluttering had begun, trying to feel it again through the petticoats. Lifegiver – that was her function. Nurturer, trainer, and fashioner. Lifegiver.

With quickening steps she started across the yard to the gate, unlatched it and passed through, heading purposefully toward the little gully where the trees had been left when the surrounding hills were cleared. Back at the house Edward raised himself from the tree-stump seat and called after her, but she kept on without turning back. He sat again and after a few moments continued his task.

At the lip of the gully she paused, then started downward among the ferns and the taller trees, stopping in a small space between the larger trunks to crouch and study the bush floor. She touched several small spikes of green growth before she selected a tiny seedling growing in a patch of light.

With her fingers she cleared the area around it, then picked up a dry twig to help loosen the earth before she scraped it away. When the little plant was free she wrapped some moss around the small ball of earth clinging to the roots and, cradling it in her cupped palms, carried it back to the house.

As she entered the yard her husband looked up. "What have you got there?"

"A seedling," she replied, "I'm going to plant it."

He shrugged slightly and resumed his work. Lydia stood for a moment watching, then crossed to the kitchen door where she stopped to pick up a cracked jug. From the vegetable garden on the north side of the house she scooped up some soil, filled the jug, and planted the small green shoot. Then she tricked a little water around it and placed it near the door where she could watch it grow.

The noise of the planing stopped. She looked over and saw Edward examining the piece of wood he held out in front of him. The coming Sunday she'd go with him up the hill to the cemetery. Three white crosses there'd be there then – among those of the soldiers and seamen killed at Gate Pa and Te Ranga.

But that one would be the last. Now she had planted the livewood, for the new life.

She felt movement again, and once more she put her hand to her waist. When the fluttering feeling stopped she bent over at the doorway and touched a tender finger to the frond of green.

The sound of the planing began again, but this time it receded into the background as she went about her work.

Deadwood Livewood was broadcast by *Radio New Zealand*, first in 1984.

ABSENT FRIENDS

The children ran out of the cottage as they heard the hooves in the yard. Henry dismounted, slipped the bridle of plaited twine from Bess' head, and let her into the enclosure that stretched from the rear of the house all the way back to the trees. At the side of the wooden building the two young apple trees he and Sarah had planted the year before were now reaching above the barrier he had erected around them to protect them from their small flock of sheep and single goat. Perhaps next year there would be fruit.

Little Jane was jumping up and down near the doorstep. She was still in her sleeping gown and the little plaits Sarah had made in her hair the evening before so she would have crinkled hair on the morrow were still tied.

"Papa, papa," she squealed, "look, an orange. There was an orange in my stocking."

William, his short legs enclosed in a pair of overlarge new trousers his mother had made by lamplight, spending most evenings over two weeks, had a slightly puzzled look on his face.

"Where did you go so early, Papa? Did you forget it's Christmas day?"

Henry leant the spade against the stand holding the water tank, and washed his hands under the tap, using the rough bar of tallow soap kept in a cracked dish on the sawn-off stump underneath it.

"How could I forget it," he asked, "with all the times you've reminded me over the past days? I just woke up early and felt like taking Bess for a ride."

Sarah appeared at the door, wiping her hands on the apron she wore over her grey dress. Time and sun had seen it fade from the darker shade it had once been. Later, with more of the preparations done and before the guests arrived, she would change into her blue second-best gown, even though the day promised to be too hot for it.

"You went for a ride with a spade?" she asked.

"There was something I needed to do."

"You haven't taken a day off all year. Surely you wouldn't work today, Henry?"

"Of course not," he replied, "there was just something I had to do." Jane handed her father her hairbrush and the two sat on the wooden slab that formed the step into the main room of the cottage. He undid the cloth ties around the ends of her plaits and began to brush them out.

Henry finally pushed his plate away and sat back. The others, his own family and the Westons who had ridden over from their neighbouring block, had all finished and were sitting, satisfied, around the temporary table the two men had erected outside. A canvas tent fly Robert Weston had brought with him, packed into a bulky sack parcel tied to the back of his saddle so it sat squarely on the horse's rump, had been rigged with two poles to stand out from the house and provide shelter from the sun. The carcasses of two roosters lay on a platter in the middle of the table, but all the other plates had been emptied.

"May we go and play now?" asked one of the children and, at a nod from the mothers, the five young ones scrambled down from their plank seating and ran to retrieve the wooden toy each had received in a small ceremony before the meal.

"Must we keep our boots on?" William stopped to ask. As his mother hesitated he added, "They pinch my toes."

"So do mine," said Edward Weston who was a like size and age to William. With their sun-bleached yellow hair and tanned skin, the two boys could have been taken for brothers.

"And mine." The cry was a chorus now. The children tugged at their boots and stockings and once again barefoot ran toward the stream to play.

The adults sat for a time without speaking, gazing at the tree-covered hills that surrounded the few acres of cleared land and the cottage.

"It gets a little easier each year, I'm thinking," Elizabeth Weston said after a few minutes.

The men agreed, but Sarah remained silent. It was her fifth Christmas in the new colony, and she still found it difficult to reconcile blue skies and heat with this time of year. She tried to imagine the scene that would be taking place in the family home so far away in Hampshire, but the idea of sitting around a roaring fire on such a day as this was incongruous. She prickled a little in her blue gown. Yet in July when a storm had battered their little home and she'd yearned then for the familiar hearth and the company of those she missed, she knew it to be just as inappropriate to the summer season her family was enjoying then. At such times the dislocation seemed irreparable. Then she remembered with a feeling almost akin to guilt the realization she had come to while writing her last letter home – she was beginning to think it was England and its seasons that were out of order rather than those of this raw new land.

To the left of the doorway into the cottage a young rimu tree stood in the spare wooden bucket. By lamplight the evening before, with the children asleep behind the curtained partition off the large room, she and Henry had hung the decorations on its weeping fronds. Over the three previous nights she had rolled small pieces of dough coloured with pūhā leaves, raupo pollen, and konini and miro berries, into different shapes, pierced them with a darning needle, dried them in the cooling stove, then threaded a loop of cotton onto each. A necklace of glass beads had been taken apart and each bead remade into a shining droplet. Thin strips of cloth were tied into bows around the narrow drooping branches. A letter from home, written last January but not reaching her hands till August, displayed her younger sister's enthusiasm and provided the inspiration. "This past Christmas we had a decorated tree in the parlour. Christmas trees have become quite the thing here – everyone has them. Since Grandpapa left us, and now even Queen Victoria is pictured with her family around their tree, Papa agreed he could see no harm in it." The decorated rimu had now been moved outside in order to make more space inside the cottage's main room and to help lend a special air to the shared dinner. To Sarah, facing it as she sat at the table, it was a somewhat disjointed link with home. She had no doubt the Hampshire parlour hosted such a tree again this year, though it was not part of her memory of past times.

Partly in order to divert her thoughts, Sarah reached out to gather the dishes from the table. The china dinner set, which spent all year in a wooden box stored under their bed, had been unpacked that morning and admired as though new. Later in the afternoon after the pieces had been washed and dried, it would be repacked for another year. She bent to pick up a wide tin pan lying on the ground beside her, and piled the plates into it. Elizabeth began to assist, even though Sarah put out a hand to restrain her.

"Now don't you fuss over me," Elizabeth had said earlier while the two women worked together to prepare the meal, "I may be in my sixth month, but I'm thinking I'm still stronger than you are."

Sarah had been relieved to hear the other woman's chuckled comment, as for some weeks now she had found herself anticipating with some trepidation her attendance at the coming confinement, wondering at her capability. Elizabeth, though, laughed at her neighbour's reaction when she first broke the news, assuring her that on two of the times before this she'd had no woman to assist at all, and having Sarah present would be preferable to having only Robert with his rough hands. Indeed, she added, she was looking forward to it for that reason. Sarah, remembering her own experiences, shuddered but then recalled the other woman's reassuring confidence on the occasion of little Jane's arrival. She knew she would not be able to repay her in like manner but was determined to do her best.

While the women were busy in the lean-to that formed the kitchen at the back of the cottage, Robert Weston lay on the flax mat spread out on the grass slope below the cottage, his hat tipped forward over his face. Beside him, Henry sat watching where further down the field that was cleared except for the largest stumps the horses could not shift, William and Jane played with their three friends. At a given point they each threw a stick into the narrow stream, then followed along the bank to the bend, calling out encouragement to their selected contestants in the race.

Henry leaned back, propping himself on his elbows so he

could still observe the children.

"You saw the Christmas tree…" it was more a statement than a question, for on the neighbours' arrival the adults had stood together watching the children's delight as they examined the decorations.

"I went out yesterday afternoon to get it," continued Henry, "and I came across something." He paused. A change in his tone made Robert open his eyes and sit up. He tipped his hat back on his head.

"I found a fallen tree. A felled tree," Henry corrected, "it had been chopped down. Someone had started to saw it up." He paused for some moments. "He was still there."

Robert stared in surprise. "Are you telling me someone else is working in this area," he asked, "without our knowing about it?"

"Not now." Henry paused again for some seconds. "It would have been a good ten years ago, I should think – well before either of us settled in this area."

"So what are you telling me? Was there someone there or not?"

"Someone, and no one anymore."

"You found a body?"

"A skeleton."

"God rest his soul. Was there anything to show who he was?"

"A rusty saw and axe – not much else left."

"Poor beggar. I wonder how he died."

Henry found it more difficult than he thought to answer, but after some hesitation described the scene to his neighbour – the partly split log, and the skeleton beside it, its right hand caught in the split.

"He must have been putting in a wedge when the end one

flew out and the split closed on his hand," he explained.

"What about his axe?"

"Out of reach. About two feet too far away, I'd say."

The two men sat together, gazing down the slope. Their eyes followed the children as they played, but each in his thoughts imagining the days that must have followed the accident years before.

"Cold drink?" The two women stood beside the pair with cups and a jug. The men moved to make room on the mat, and the four sat together under the blue sky. Sarah raised her cup.

"Here's to the families we left behind."

"And to our own families here," said Elizabeth.

"To family and friends near and far," added Robert.

Henry raised his cup and saluted the bush-line before he drank.

"To family and friends, present and far," he said. "And absent friends."

ROCKING THE CRADLE

The telegram from Kate telling Anne the news arrived just before midday. She called out to Bessie who was cleaning the three guest rooms, and the two of them sat down at the scrubbed kitchen table and toasted the victory with a glass of the lemonade Bessie had made the day before and stored in the ventilated box on the cool south side of the kitchen.

"We'll take the rest of the day off, in celebration," Anne said, adding as she noted the other's anxious look that she'd be paid for it. Bessie took off her apron, put on her hat, and started the two-mile walk home, glad to have the extra hour's start on her own chores. After feeding the baby, Anne tucked him into the perambulator and spent the afternoon visiting.

When Arthur arrived home with the copy of the evening news that bore the precious headline, the dinner was almost ready, as usual.

"Look at that," he said, throwing the newspaper onto the table so the men who were the current paying guests could see it.

Mr Tomkins got up from his chair and looked out the window. Mr Houghton pulled his eyeglasses from his nose and polished them vigorously. Anne wondered if her husband was being insensitive, or whether he'd forgotten that neither of their older lodgers could read much more than their own names. She picked up the paper and read aloud.

"Women's Franchise Bill Passed. His Excellency, the Governor, yesterday signed the Electoral Bill allowing womanhood suffrage."

"Would you believe it?" asked Arthur, "they passed the bill. They really did it. It's been all the talk at the club today. You know what this means don't you? Now every woman has as much say in the running of the country as does a man."

"I doubt that," said Mr Houghton. "After all, women aren't interested in such things. They'll simply vote the way their husbands tell them to."

"That's right," agreed Tomkins, "what it means is that married men will have twice the vote that single men have."

"That's what John Hall intends," said Arthur, "to increase the influence of the settler and the family man, in order to overcome that of the single man."

"Loafers and drunkards, all of us, according to Hall," growled Mr Houghton. "The man has a bally cheek – er, excuse me, missus."

"I thought Seddon had more sense," said Mr Tomkins. "All that past talk about women's place being in the home, and the danger of power unsexing them. He stopped it before, and now he's given way and let the bill go through. Lost his nerve, he has. What sort of a leader is it who bows to pressure from a bunch of women?

Anne looked up from the saucepan of cabbage she was draining. So far, the youngest of her lodgers hadn't said a word.

"And you, Mr Newman? Do you think women should have the same right as men to have a say in the governing of the country?"

The young man looked distinctly uncomfortable. "I'm not sure that it's up to me to say."

"And why not, Mr Newman?" asked Anne, tipping the cabbage into a bowl and placing it over the range to keep it warm. "You voted in the last election, I presume. Do you think your sisters should have the same right?"

The young man stared down at the table, his right hand fiddling with the edge of the starched linen cloth.

"Edith, my older sister," he paused, and Anne noticed his ears reddening as he said, "she sent me a pamphlet that women in Christchurch are distributing..."

"Pamphlets," scorned Tomkins, "waste of time. Why do women think they can vote better than men?"

"Not necessarily better than men," responded Anne, "women want the right to vote as well as men – that is, alongside men."

"As well as men," Mr Houghton exploded, ignoring the added explanation. "How can they vote as well as men when they are completely ignorant of the duties and responsibilities of public life?"

Mr Newman, rather surer of himself when he could quote arguments put forward by others, started again.

"The pamphlet listed many reasons why women believe they should be able to choose the government…"

"Women believe!" Once again his words were cut short. "Women might believe they are capable, but the fact is they just don't know. Women who have never done a day's work in their lives – how can they possibly be fit to have a say in how the country is run?"

Anne looked at her husband, but Arthur had picked up the newspaper and was reading, apparently deaf to the discussion going on around him. Mr Houghton continued.

"And not all women are in favour anyway. It's only a handful of wild women who make a noise to make the country think that all women actually want to vote. The matter has never been put to the country."

Arthur looked up from the pages of the paper.

"It says here that more than thirty thousand women signed the last electoral petition. Would you believe it? Fancy that. Just fancy." He returned to his reading, oblivious to the timeliness of his contribution. Mr Houghton polished his eyeglasses again.

"Nearly thirty-two thousand, as I understand it," said Anne, "and it was not the first petition."

Mr Newman looked up, his mouth opened then closed again. He went back to his study of the tablecloth. Mr Tomkins watched as Anne unlatched the door of the range oven and stooped to remove the large pan holding the roast.

"I can only wonder what my mother, God rest her soul, would have thought of it," he said, almost to himself.

"Was your mother a person, Mr Tomkins?" Anne asked with a smile as she lifted the meat and held it above the pan to drip.

The man gave her a look that suggested he had just provided justification for his point of view. "Of course she was."

"But the former Electoral Bill stated 'Person does not include female.'" Was she mistaken, or did a slight smile appear on the lips of Mr Newman? Arthur was still engrossed in his reading, and Mr Houghton was standing in the doorway with his back to her, but the hands clasped behind him were clenching and unclenching in turn.

"Was your mother a criminal, or a lunatic?"

"Certainly not." Mr Tomkins' tone betrayed his annoyance at the question.

"Then don't you think," asked Anne, transferring the vegetables to a serving dish, "that since she was subject to the law she should have had the right to a voice in the framing of the laws?" No immediate answer came from Mr Tomkins, so Anne continued. "I would have thought that you would not be happy to see her placed along with aliens, minors, and idiots."

This time there was no doubt. Mr Newman grinned, but immediately put up a hand to hide it and turned his head away from the older man. Mr Tomkins let several seconds elapse before replying.

"It's not that I think women are not fit to vote, but that they have too much to lose if they do."

Anne paused, the dish in her hand poised over the table.

"And what is it they would lose, Mr Tomkins?"

The man looked surprised at the question. "Why, their femininity of course. Women shouldn't be involved in the politics of elections, it's unwomanly, it will demoralize them. I don't believe any sensible woman would take up the right to attend at polling booths with men."

"It's the anti-liquor movement behind it all that's to blame, it's obvious," said Mr Houghton. "Those temperance women and the wowsers. If they get their way no decent working man will be able to get a drink."

Arthur let out a hoot of laughter. He held up the newspaper and waved it at the other men.

"Look at this letter," he said, jabbing a finger at the centre of the page. "Read it for yourself." He thrust it forward. Mr Tomkins turned to gaze out the window again. Arthur pushed the paper in the direction of Mr Newman. The young man took it and began to read.

"Aloud, aloud," commanded Arthur.

"Despite your correspondent 'Head of the Family's' repetition of the frequently-repeated charge that 'the women of this country do not clamour for support of the enfranchisement of their sex', the women of New Zealand have recently arisen to demonstrate their support in unprecedented numbers. I would remind your readers that the petition now before the House is but the most recent of six submitted over the past eight years. To those men who fear that the actions of women who have pursued this goal are unwomanly…"

"The words of one of the shrieking sisters herself," roared Arthur, shaking with delight. "Carry on."

"…it should be pointed out that had men, who regard themselves as the protectors of women, themselves conducted the campaign for the rights of their mothers, wives, and sisters, such measures undertaken by women would not have been necessary. Hy-pat… Hy-pat…"

"Hypatia," Anne put in, then looked at each of the men to see if they had picked up on her clarification. Only Mr Newman appeared to have noticed. He gave her a glance before dropping his eyes to the printed page.

Arthur roared with laughter again. "Well, you have to allow them that point," he said. "So now we have only ourselves to blame if we end up with petticoat government.

The hand that was stirring the pan of gravy stopped in its movement for a moment, then resumed its circular motion. Mr Houghton turned and strode forward two paces to slap his hand on the table.

"It is because men are the protectors of women that we want to protect them from this madness. Women are already represented by their fathers, their husbands, and their sons. They are dependent on men, therefore they should not vote."

Arthur leant back in his chair, his hands clasped behind his head. Anne looked at her husband, imagining him occupying that pose for most of the day.

"But, Mr Houghton," she asked, pouring the gravy into a crockery jug and setting it on the table, "what about women who earn their own living, and pay taxes? There are forty-five thousand women in New Zealand who are tax-payers." She thought about the reason why she continued to have paying guests in her house after she married, and looked at her husband again. Arthur's chair tilted even further onto its back legs. Alarmingly far.

Mr Houghton's hand again thumped down on the table. "Mark my words," he said, "if women get the vote…"

"Now women have the vote," corrected Anne, but the older man continued.

"If women get the vote they will become man's rival rather than his supporter."

Anne opened her mouth to reply, but Mr Houghton turned and walked from the room. She heard him go out the back door to the tank-stand, turn on the tap and splash water over his hands. She picked up the saucepan containing the white sauce. There was a problem with the consistency. With a wooden spoon she blended in a further teaspoon of flour, poured it over the cauliflower then grated nutmeg over it.

Mr Newman got up to help her transfer the serving dishes to the table. Arthur removed the newspaper. He pointed at the letter again, shaking his head in amusement. "Petticoat government," he repeated, and tucked the paper under the cushion of his chair before sitting again.

The baby cried out in the adjacent room, and Anne went in to attend to him. As she changed his napkin she heard Arthur saying the grace – "For what we are about to receive, may the Lord make us truly thankful."

"Amen," responded the other men, and the clink of cutlery began.

Anne put the baby down again and tucked the blanket

around him.

"A–men," she said to her son, and stood rocking the cradle gently from side to side.

1900s early decades

The early decades of the 1900s were years of great expansion as trade with the northern hemisphere increased. The population grew very quickly as immigrants flowed in from Great Britain, other parts of Europe, and Australia. With the annexation of Pacific Island groups, the Dominion of New Zealand declared, national sports teams competing overseas, and citizens achieving international renown in fields of scholarship and invention, the character of the nation was being forged.

On the less favourable side, many thousands of lives were lost as Kiwi soldiers fought in World War l and World War ll, in support of the British Empire. The usage of the term 'Kiwi' to refer to New Zealanders dates from the time of WWl.

The country also suffered from the worldwide influenza epidemic in 1918, the great depression of the 1930s, and two severe earthquakes.

WE THAT ARE LEFT GROW OLD

Oh, the stories that went around. So many. You didn't know which of them to believe.

A farmer went out one morning to check on some stock, dropped dead, and wasn't found for days – his wife and son too sick with the flu to get out of bed to look for him, if they even knew he'd gone. Plenty of tales of people waking in the morning feeling well, and then dead by nightfall. Children orphaned when their parents died – that's if the little ones didn't succumb too. Bodies turning black like they did with the pneumonia. Even if only half of the stories we heard were true it was too horrible to think about. It was a terrible time.

And right when we were all hoping that the war was coming to an end, and the men – those of them that hadn't been killed like our Sydney – would be coming home.

Eleanor got it first – that was in September. She put it down to being sneezed on by someone standing by her desk at the solicitor's office. She was in bed for a week, and I didn't get to see her for all that time and another week afterward, because my mother wouldn't let me come anywhere near her. She shifted me out of the room that Eleanor and I shared, into the parlour at the front of the house, and made me wear a bag of camphor around my neck. I thought everyone at school would complain at the smell, but it turned out that lots of others were wearing them too.

The day Eleanor went back to work was the day I came down

with it. By then, the school roll was down to half. Not many pupils escaped the flu that year. Poor Mum. She'd just finished nursing one daughter through it, and she had to begin again with the other. Mothers don't get sick, she said, they don't have time to.

That was wrong though, because by the time it was all over we knew of lots of mothers who had, and quite a few who died.

Eleanor was back at work for a couple of weeks when they closed the office. Mr Stanwick had been taken bad, and because of the epidemic, which was what they were calling it then, many shops and businesses had shut too because they didn't have the staff to run them.

It turned out we were lucky we got it early, Eleanor and me. Those who picked it up later got it worse. If we thought it was bad before, the epidemic was much more severe a few weeks further on.

By then, there was a public health order that schools in the district had to close – there was hardly anyone attending anyway. After that they closed all sorts of public places where people got together. Council workmen went around spraying the main streets in town, and in some spots they had rooms, or machines, where you could breathe in some gas in the hope it would kill the flu germs before they killed you.

What with all who were sick, and others who were trying to keep themselves away so they wouldn't get it, as well as the ban, there weren't many people around.

Except at the hospital, of course. It was overrun. All the wards were full and two marquees were set up on the lawn – one for women, the other for men, though I think that after a time that wasn't adhered to strictly. People got put wherever a space could be found, and none of the patients was in a fit state to worry who was on the stretcher next to them. Of course the doctors and nurses were coming down with the flu too, so not only were there far too many patients, but not nearly enough staff.

When the call went out for volunteers, Eleanor and Mum didn't hesitate. I was too young, they said – my job was to stay at home and keep things running there for when they came back to eat and sleep. If I needed any help I should ask Mr or Mrs Dubicki next door. Some nights I didn't see them, Mum or Eleanor, and when they did appear they'd drop into bed with hardly a word, sleep a few hours, then go off out again. When I asked anything about it, they'd tell me not to worry, it would be over soon. But each day it seemed the bells on the ambulances barely stopped ringing through the streets. I stopped going out the front gate as much as I could, so as to avoid the sight of a car or truck parked in front of houses along the block, and men with masks over their faces lifting a sheet-covered form and loading it into the vehicle.

Mr Dubicki kept me up to date about what was going on in Europe. His index finger would draw lines on the map pinned on their kitchen wall, pointing out where the British Army were advancing, and talking about places I'd heard of at Sunday school – Jordan, Judea, Nazareth, Damascus. He talked of the Ottoman empire, Kaiser Wilhelm, King Ferdinand, David Lloyd George, and other names I couldn't pronounce. On the day that he grabbed my hands and tried to tell me that Poland had declared its independence from Russia I hardly heard the excitement in his voice – I'd come to tell Mrs Dubicki that Mum had been sent home in a taxi and was really bad, aching all over and vomiting.

Together we nursed her – taking turns to feed her spoons of

soup, cool her when the fever was at its worst, changing her nightgown and sheets, propping her up with pillows so she could breathe more easily, and rubbing her back to encourage her to cough up the phlegm.

I was sent along to the chemist shop to see if there was anything I could get to help her, but the chemist just shook his head. They were even out of painkillers for the headache. Just make sure she doesn't get up too soon, he said, some people think they're getting better then they come down with pneumonia and… He shook his head again, not finishing the sentence.

It came at last – Armistice Day. Eleanor arrived home from the hospital sometime in the early hours but, even though she wasn't due back at the hospital till late afternoon, she insisted on getting up at nine o'clock and biking into town. I'm not going to miss this, she said, it's been long enough coming. She came back in the early afternoon holding a paper bag with two currant buns, and a paper flag. We had a bun each with a cup of tea, then took some soup into Mum and got about a half of a cup down her throat. It was the most she had in one go for some time.

It's Peace, Mum, Eleanor said. Peace at last. Did you hear the church bells ringing? Mum managed a small smile.

I went and got the flag from the kitchen and put it in her hands as she lay there. She smiled again and moved her hand so the Union Jack waved in celebration. I knew at that moment that she'd get better. No matter how long it took, she'd be one of the lucky ones.

GUESTS

In 1937 my birthday fell on a Saturday. My cake was half a loaf of bread with a candle on top, and I learned a new word.

I wasn't expecting a present – there was no money for anything like that. Three weeks before the day Mum had remade a woollen dress that belonged to Aunt Ngaire. She unpicked the seams, cut it down, and sewed it up again on the treadle machine that was one of the few things we'd brought with us from the city. The dress was to be my birthday present, but when we had a cold snap a week before the date Mum hurried the hand finishing and gave it to me early. My cotton frock was thin and now too short, so I was glad to have a warmer one to wear to school.

I was lucky we'd been able to keep the sewing machine when most of our other belongings were sold. Some of my classmates came to school in clothes that were far too big for them – adult sizes hanging on small bodies. It was either that or not come at all, and sometimes the latter was the only option – at least when rain ruled out weekend washdays.

Mum might have had a word with the teachers, or perhaps it was the other way around, because on a few occasions when a child came regularly in a dress or trousers so large and ill-fitting they couldn't run and play they were sent off down our road with a note. Back they'd come later in the day with the garment remade into something more serviceable, and when I went home after school there'd be off-cuts of the material on the table. Any sizeable scraps left over from sewing were stitched together to make bedcovers, and one of my most lasting memories of those times was the assorted colours and textures of the blankets on my bed.

Sometimes Mum did small sewing jobs for other people. She didn't charge because she said she'd had no training and didn't know how to do the finishing touches as the professionals did. Nobody had cash for such things anyway. But within a week or so of her working at the machine, a child would arrive with a bag of plums, or there'd be a pumpkin on the doorstep in the morning. That's the way people looked out for each other then. I knew that next summer my outgrown cotton frock would appear again at school on a smaller girl. Somehow everyone made do. More or less.

My new dress was of aqua-coloured wool and had small darts under the arms. I didn't need them yet, but Mum always made allowance for growth and as she fitted it on me she said

"You'll be filling out soon," and sighed.

I knew she was worried about what would happen when I finished primary school. She desperately wanted me to go on to the district high school, but that would mean the loss of the little money I might earn from working. On the other hand, there was almost no chance of my finding work anyway, especially in the rural area we'd moved to when we left the city.

Most days, Dad helped out on a farm two miles up the road. It wasn't often he earned cash, but Mr Gill kept us supplied with meat. Each Saturday morning he'd kill a sheep and unless it was a really lean week Dad would go and pick up a fore-quarter or hind-quarter, so there was mutton for the three of us from Sunday through to about Wednesday, or even Thursday depending on the weather because we had no way of keeping it fresh in summer. It was a good deal for Mr Gill as most of the time he couldn't sell the meat anyway, and it was good for us. As well as that, each day Dad did work he'd bring home a bucket of milk. That helped supplement the fifteen shillings a week Dad got for being a married man on the dole.

What with that and the vegetable garden we coped reasonably well for food, though there was no money for more than the occasional variation from the standard bread, meat, and the vegetables we grew ourselves. Potatoes, kūmara, carrots, cabbages, cauliflowers, tomatoes, silverbeet, beans, and peas all flourished under Mum's care. Sometimes we gathered cress from the stream, Dad and I picked mushrooms in season, and pūhā grew wild everywhere. Fruit trees planted on the property and along some roads years before and largely neglected since, nevertheless bore well and any excess was made into sauces and preserves. With the help of parsley, chives, mint, rosemary and other herbs grown in a separate plot near the tank stand, Mum made each meal, no matter how plain otherwise, full of flavour and aromatic. We were well off compared to some. I tried to remember that whenever I thought about the chocolate and the other sweet treats Grandad used to give me on special occasions. I missed him.

Whenever we felt the pinch either Mum or Dad would say "We're lucky we moved from the city when we did – imagine what it would be like if we had to pay rent."

When Dad's job finally disappeared almost two years earlier, there were no savings left to fall back on. For the eighteen months before that his hours had been cut back several times so the money put away for a deposit on a house had been eaten up.

"No one can afford professional services," said Dad "and who needs an accountant when nobody has any money or assets left." For the first month he walked from firm to firm in the hope of finding employment. The next month he added factories. After that he even tried for labouring jobs. The furniture was sold piece by piece.

"Are things any better back in England?" I heard Mum ask him one day. "You could go back home, to your family there, till the depression's over."

"No," he replied, "I've told you, I'm a New Zealander now. I won't go back. Besides, I'm not leaving you and Jean."

When we could no longer afford the rent on our house, it was Mum who suggested we move from the city, even though she'd be leaving behind her own family. Dad had never lived in the country, and the landlord would probably not have forced us out because by then he knew he couldn't let the house to anyone else anyway and he preferred to see someone in it who would look after it. But with little furniture left and no hope of the situation improving, Dad knew, better than most, that the shift was the better alternative, and a more comfortable move for him than remaining in the city with no position or standing.

The place we moved into was built as a farm-worker's house; one long main room in the middle, which was living-room and kitchen, with a narrow room off each end which served as bedrooms – my parents' on one side and mine on the other. Dad had insisted on keeping the beds.

"At least we won't be reduced to sleeping on the floor like animals," he said. But somehow, in the move, the end board of mine disappeared, so the frame holding my wire-wove was held up at the bottom by two tree stumps. They were solid supports and did the job well but were cut a bit too high, so the foot of my bed was a couple of inches higher than the head.

On the day before my birthday Mum made a cake with two eggs from a neighbour's hens, and a handful of saved sultanas.

We were going to have it the following night after dinner. Gran was coming from the city next day on the bus, because her own birthday was within a week of mine and it was the first one for both of us since Grandad died. It was to be a small party – just the four of us. We didn't have guests very often, and never overnight – there wasn't the room in our little place and people weren't travelling much anyway – except the men who appeared at the door asking if we had any work for them to do. But Gran was going to stay over for the one night. She would have my bed while I slept on the floor in the living room.

Dad left on Saturday morning to walk into town to meet the service car. He set out a good hour and a half early because on the way he had to go to Mr Gill's farm for the meat – he had a sugar-sack pikau to carry it in. Then he and Gran had a three-mile walk back home. Mum and I made up my bed for Gran and I went along the road to see if there were any wildflowers left to put in a jar in her room. The cold snap had had its effect on the weeds along the roadside because I wasn't finding much that would look good enough.

The grass on the verge was long, so it wasn't till I was almost on top of him that I saw the man lying down. His feet were just inches away from the ridge of shingle at the edge of the road. His face was turned to the side, away from me, and he didn't move. I stood and looked down at him for half a minute or so, then I touched his boot lightly with my own. There was no response. At the second nudge he shifted, then lifted his head.

"I'm sorry," I said, "I didn't know if…"

He nodded. "That's all right," he said, "I'm not sure myself sometimes." I didn't know what to say next. He sighed and sat up.

"Is there somewhere I can get some water?"

"We live just up the road," I said, "we can let you have water."

He pulled himself up and his clothes hung even more loosely on him when he was standing than when lying down. Together we walked back along the road, him unsure on his feet, neither of us saying a word.

Mother was washing some dishes in the enamel bowl. She looked around as I spoke.

"Mum, this man wants some water." I saw her face change. From surprise, to fear, and then to something else in the moments it took for her to take in the sight, because by now I was steadying the man by holding his arm.

"Gordon…" I thought I heard her say, almost under her breath, and wondered for an instant if she knew him. It wasn't till that night, thinking about it in the dark on my own, that I realized I almost heard my mother utter a phrase she'd have winced to hear anyone else say – she a lay-preacher's daughter.

She came to the door and stretched out her hand. With me pushing on one arm and her pulling on the other, we helped the stranger up the step into the house and sat him down in Dad's chair at the table.

"Quickly," she said, thrusting the water bucket into my hand. I went out the back and half-filled it from the tap on the tank.

When a glass of water was in his hand Mum filled the kettle, put it on the hob, and put another piece of wood in the fire. Then she opened the cupboard and took out one of the loaves she'd baked that morning. She cut a thick slice, spread it with mutton dripping and put the plate in front of the man.

At the time I thought maybe he didn't want it because he just sat there and looked at it. I suppose I imagined that someone as hungry as he appeared to be would have grabbed it and stuffed it in his mouth, but he didn't – he just sat there and looked at it. Mum put the bucket back in my hand and sent me out again for more water though I was sure we didn't need it yet. When I came back he was chewing slowly, and there was another slab on the plate – this one spread with the jam we'd made when the blackberries were ripe. There wasn't much of it because we couldn't afford the sugar, so it was kept for Sunday tea.

He ate deliberately, stopping from time to time and closing his eyes for a minute or so. At the bench Mum kept herself occupied with taking plates out of the cupboards and replacing them. Twice more she placed bread in front of him, once as a sandwich with nasturtium leaves and a little homemade cheese inside. It seemed a long time before he finished. Mum poured him another cup of tea then she filled her own cup and sat down at the table with him.

"We haven't got much room here, as you can see, but you're welcome to stay a while if you like," she said.

The man spoke for the first time since he'd been inside the house, apart from a small acknowledgement when another plate had been put down. I thought for a moment he was going to cry, but he cleared his throat and said,

"Thank you very much, but I've got to get on."

Mum renewed the invitation, but the man replied that it was important that he got to Hamilton as soon as he could. Mother sipped her tea, and after a few moments the man continued.

"When things got bad and we had to leave the house my wife took our two boys up to stay with her parents. I've been travelling around trying to find work – haven't had any for some weeks now." He stopped for a while, as though he had used up his strength for the time being. "About a week ago I got news that the little one, our Peter, had caught chicken pox. He never was a strong boy." Again he stopped. When he began again the words came with a rush. "Because I wasn't settled in one place,

I didn't get the letter till three weeks after Mary wrote it. He's been gone a month now."

Mum put her hand on his arm.

"It's another three or four days walk," she said, "do you think..."

"I might be lucky enough to get a lift – I got one a couple of days ago."

"Just sit a while longer," said Mum, "I'll pack something up for you." She went back to the bench, and I could see her looking in the cupboard. Because it was Saturday there was no meat. We picked vegetables from the garden as we needed them so there were no cooked leftovers. She sent me out to pull some carrots and get a couple of apples from the lean-to storage area Dad had added to the back wall of the house. She put them into a washed cotton flour-bag, with the other fresh loaf of bread. That meant she'd have to get up early tomorrow morning and make another before breakfast. She always baked a double lot on Saturday so she didn't have to do it on Sunday, and so there'd be more time for the meat to roast before dinner.

The cupboard door was ajar, and I saw my cake on the shelf. I took it down and held it out to her. She hesitated just for a moment, then opened the bag for me to put it in. Together we handed the man the bag and a bottle of tea. That was the second time I had seen tears in a man's eyes.

Later that night, lying on my makeshift mattress of coats on the floor in the living room, I heard Mum crying softly in the next room.

"Jack," she was saying, "he was emaciated. Emaciated."

Guests was commended in the International Writers' Workshop short story competition 2003; and published in *This Side of the World* anthology 2007.

COMING HOME

Each time the train stopped on the way up the island the scenes were repeated. With variations.

Men jumped down, or lowered themselves less nimbly, some with the aid of sticks or crutches, to be claimed by groups of people waiting – kisses from the women, handshakes from the men. Small children were plucked from the platform and swung by khaki-clad arms above the heads of the crowds.

At Dannevirke, a lance corporal Reg had met on the ship home had his wooden crutch snatched away by a lad who must have been a young brother, while four older men hoisted him high on their shoulders. He was borne off the platform amid a throng of tall fair people, toward a truck decorated with flowers and ribbons.

The crowd on the station at Waipukurau had divided itself into two. The first group was packed with people in dark clothes – old stooped women with shark-tooth earrings dangling, men leaning on carved walking sticks, a knot of younger women, with children at each side. As the train drew to a stop the men aboard could hear the strains of a melody and saw tears coursing down the cheeks of the women. Further down the platform the dresses of the women in the second group made splashes of bright colours against the men's dark suits. Children jumped up and down in excitement, and handkerchiefs were raised to dab at over-brimming eyes. The size of the crowd delayed the descent of the dozen or so soldiers who were waiting to alight.

As each appeared at the door, a short blessing and welcome was uttered by an elderly man holding the most ornate of the carved sticks.

There were fewer left in the carriage when the train pulled out of the station again. Reg looked around and saw that those remaining appeared to be settling back to their thoughts. One to his right had his eyes closed but a thin line of water tracked down his left cheek. As Reg glanced across, a khaki-clad sleeve brushed it away. He leaned back and stared out the window to his left.

Green. It was so green. Various shades, to be sure, but green everywhere. He remembered, how long ago was it, telling a young woman in Italy, as much as the limited words they had in common would allow, about how green was his home country. In the end he pointed to her emerald scarf, then waved his arm across the panorama "Like this," he said, "green – New Zealand is all green."

Now, gazing at it anew, he felt a thrill of recognition pass through him. He had been right. Those endless days in the camp, four hundred and forty one days of waiting, wasted days of mindless limbo, some of sickness of body, all of boredom, when in order to relieve the grey monotony of the days he would lie on his bunk, close his eyes, and remember the landscape of home. Recalling in as much detail as he could the line of the hills behind the house, the trees, even the shapes of the leaves on trees almost as far away around the world as it was possible to be. Sometimes he stopped to wonder if his imagining made it all greener and fresher than it really was. And during those weeks on the ship coming home, when all there was to see in every direction was water, he would stand near the bow looking ahead and thinking that every mile was bringing him closer to home, he had wondered again. But here it was unrolling before him, acre upon acre, mile upon mile.

The train passed over a bridge and looking down Reg saw two channels of silver sparkling their way through stretches of grey stones. On the banks, last summer's stalks of toetoe, now greying and tattered, inclined stiffly in the wind. Soon the new spikes would rise and produce the fluffy blond heads to bow and straighten as breezes ruffled their locks – just as he had pictured them so many times standing against the blue of the sky.

Two men got up, put on their caps, and hoisted their bags onto their shoulders. As they made their way through the carriage they called out farewells. One, who Reg recalled standing by at the rails of the ship watching some of their company disembark at Lyttleton two days before, gave him a nod "See you, mate." "Good luck," he replied, as the brakes took hold and the train slowed.

On the platform two boys detached themselves from the grasp of the adults and ran forward peering into the windows as they passed, their faces glowing with excitement. Looking out, Reg saw a blur of brown as a tall form leapt from the train toward a small knot of people standing in front of the ticket office. A woman and the small girl she was holding both disappeared in an enveloping hug which was interrupted only briefly for a quick kiss to be planted on the older woman's face. An older man stood by smiling, self-conscious.

When Jack left the train at Palmerston North Reg couldn't see the people who met him. He had turned down Jack's suggestion that he get off to meet the family before he continued his journey, and the crush on the platform was so dense he could see only those right outside the window. In the three and a half years they'd been in the same company they'd come to know each other's families intimately through their shared stories but somehow, when the time came, Reg was loath to share the moment. The two men clasped hands as they parted, and Jack reminded him of their promise to get the families together as soon as possible. How glad he felt that when he did eventually meet Jack's wife it would be in this way, because they were both home safely, and not the other scenario he had reluctantly considered in his mind on far too many occasions.

Now, looking at the scene outside, Reg recalled pledges made in distant places. The Jeans and Margarets who were to be visited in fulfilment of a vow, the parents to be consoled with the knowledge that their son was one of the best, whatever the truth.

His thoughts skimmed ahead of the train, anticipating the scene further up the tracks. By now his parents would be in the old Essex, he presumed they still had it, pulling out of the farm gate onto the main road. They'd turn down Herehere Road to pick up Yvonne and little Peter – or perhaps Eileen and Ray had collected them already. Or was it a working day in which case Yvonne would be at the tearooms serving scones and cups of tea, and little Pete would now be playing with his cousins? No, he was sure she'd have arranged the day off.

It was dusk on Sunday when the ship had reached Lyttleton. The South Islanders were all packed and ready to leave but the ship didn't enter the harbour, so they settled down for another night aboard thinking they'd be sailing in the following morning. Some of them jokingly growled about another night of enforced celibacy, others who had to travel on to further destinations were partially mollified by the prospect of continuing their journey in daylight. Next morning, however, the ship stayed still, and the captain announced they were refused entry as it was Labour Day. The protests from the Christchurch men particularly were full and graphic.

"Four years and twenty-eight days," stormed a man Reg knew as Dave, "fourteen hundred and eighty nine bloody days fighting for my country and they won't let me back into the goddam place." Despite the complaints it was not till Tuesday morning that they had tied up and could again set foot on the long anticipated ground.

Another day to Wellington where he'd had a half-hour with his cousin Gwen during her break from the engineering factory in Kent Terrace, more impatient waiting, then onto the train. Did that make it Thursday or Friday? After all this time it was hard to be certain.

The willows fringing the low-lying area to the right of the train were bright green with new leaf. By now the cars, the Essex and Ray's Vauxhall, had probably reached the station and people would be gathering on the platform looking along the line for a first glimpse of the engine. It hadn't been that way the time before. He remembered that it was in the kitchen of his grandmother's house in Heretaunga Street where he had met his father. He had woken to find his mother was not beside him in the double bed and had gone into the kitchen to find a strange man at the table, his mother on his knee.

"Reggie, this is your father," said his mother, "didn't I tell you he'd come back one day."

The man got up from the chair, towering over him, and Reg stood there, his neck bent right back as he looked up at the scarred face, till she prompted, "Say hello to your father," and pushed him forward. The man held out his right hand so he put his forward too and the two had shaken hands solemnly.

Then the man picked up the khaki hat from the table and put it on Reg's head. It covered his head to his nose so he couldn't see, and he heard the two of them laugh. He snatched it off and heard his mother say as he ran from the room, "It won't take long. You'll get to know each other all over again. It'll be just like before."

But it wasn't, not for a long time. From then on, he wasn't his mother's little man. She said he was grown up now and didn't need her so much anymore. And he slept in the little room at the back of the house while that man, the one she said was his father, had the double bed with her.

Two brothers who Reg knew as Grant and Bruce Jackson, who had been sitting together at the front of the carriage, stood and began to ready themselves for arrival. Reg had met them on the ship home and found they had all gone to the same primary school and for three years had lived just four blocks away on the same street.

"Just about there," called Grant, and Reg pulled himself up from the seat and reached for his hat.

The two men stepped down before him, to be greeted by shrieks from a pair of women with deep auburn hair who flung their arms around one then the other and pulled them away to the left. For a moment Reg saw only a sea of faces without recognizing any, then a hand waved from behind the shoulder of an elderly man in front and Yvonne squeezed through a gap and was in his arms. Then the others were all around him, his mother, father, Eileen and Ray and two girls who must be Sandra and Sheryl but twice as tall as he remembered them.

There was a tug at his belt and he looked down to see a tow-haired boy looking up at him with a solemn expression. He freed his hand from around his wife's waist and was about to thrust it toward the boy. A scene from the past flashed before him. Dropping to one knee he held out both arms and enveloped the lad, holding him close. The boy wriggled, and Reg's hat was lifted from his head. He looked up to find it perched sideways on little Pete's head, and the boy was giggling with delight.

Coming Home was broadcast on *Radio New Zealand*, first in 2003 with many subsequent repeats.

TE MATAKITE

Soon she will be coming. Then will these old woman's eyes see her – the child of the daughter of this body.

Soon will the bus slow to a stop beside the store, and down she will get, Ani, barely stiff after the three hours ride. Then climbing this hill, suitcase and guitar bumping against lean brown legs. Eiee, that guitar – what evenings there will be. Just like the old times.

Too old these eyes now to pick up the service car winding down the hill into the valley. Younger they were then, when Hana it was who came. Then they could see it coming – first the cloud of dust rising behind the old bus to cover the ferns with a grey cloak till the next rain. Down the hill to meet her then – young ones in front, yelling, excited. And up they would all come again, laughing – little brothers fighting to carry the guitar. Hana then, Ani now, but the guitar the same.

Then the days of her holidays. Good times they were. Fine days digging for pipi, visiting with the uncles and aunties and their children, her kaihana, preparing meals for the large family. Loved those meals did Hana. "Real food this," she'd say. "In Wellington they don't know how to eat." Laughed then she. "Got to come home every holidays to eat up big, or I'll lose my figure."

And the evenings, the best time of all. Told us stories of the Teachers' College then – eiee she made us laugh. And the guitar. Always the guitar.

Until the last time. Quieter then was Hana, and the boy

beside her. No talk this time of coming home. No teasing of the young ones, the tāina and the tungane, or the kaihana about teaching them next year. Married then Hana, and staying in Poneke. Coming only for weddings of the tāina, and once for her father's tangi. Came with her that time did Ani – tall for her age at eight. Mokopuna but a stranger, unused to these ways.

Came once more, did Hana. For the last time. Came home for good this time. With her father now, and the tūpuna, further up the hill.

That Hine-Nui, she came for the wrong one. Better that she had taken the older and left the younger. Better it had been Hana who was left – Hana, who should be here to lead the karanga when it is my time. Now Hana is gone, and the tāina all spread across the country. Who then to make the call when Hine-Nui comes for this old one? Ani, she is coming, but she is of the new ways, not the old.

Visited here last year, did Ani, and then again – came to see the school. Like her mother she, but thinner. And the guitar. Like her mother there too – me he korokoro tui.

Soon she will be coming. Coming to teach the children of the kaihana at the school.

Dimly now can these ears hear the sound of the engine, and the huge tyres on the road. Soon she will be climbing this hill. Just like the times before, it will be, when it was Hana who came. But now none of the tamariki here to run at her side. Alone she will come.

What then is this sight that these old eyes can see? Comes now the girl, carrying the suitcase and guitar. But comes too another, walking a little behind. Clearer now is the girl as she walks closer, and with the smile of Hana on her face. Dim, though, still the other. Back she stands, near the kawakawa by the gate, watching as we two greet with the hongi.

Auē! Hine-Nui-Te-Pō it is who comes with the mokopuna. Standing she, by the gate, watching. Auē – not for the young one, e Hine. Better that you come for the old. Fading now, the vision, and the girl speaking, troubled.

"What is the matter Nanny? Why are you crying?"

"E Ani. Better perhaps that you stay in Poneke..."

Not listen though, the girl, but kisses my cheek and turns to the house. Tell her not about Hine-Nui. Tell her not that the one of darkness came with her to this place. She is not of these ways and would not understand what these old eyes have seen.

Into the house now to get the meal. E Hine – not again for the young when this old one is waiting.

* * * * * * *

Harvested now the crops, and the corn and the kūmara stored away. And Ani learning fast the ways of the tūpuna. Dig for the pipi we, together, and dive for the kōura, she. Eiee a good day that, when first she dived – came up with the kōura clutched tight in both hands, brown eyes shining. Too small it was for keeping, but proud of it, the girl, because it was the first. Then stood she on the crayfish rock, holding it above the sea.

"For Tangaroa," she said, "I return it to Tangaroa," letting it drop, and laughing as it sank into the depths, long legs waving. "I'll come back for you when you're grown up."

Teaching she, at the school. Teaching the mokopuna of the kaihana. And the kaihana not making it easy for her to begin with. "That Hana," they say, "better that she had brought the girl back to learn the real ways here, than stay in the city." But this old one tells them to hush, for Ani she is of her father's people too. So teaching the mokopuna now to speak her father's tongue, and learning from them that of her mother.

Warmth she has brought back to this home, and warmth to this heart. And in the evenings questioning, and listening. A long time since there was one who was content to listen to the old stories. So long that many of the details take a while to return. But waits she till the memories come back to this old head, and writes them down. And the kaihana they say that she is telling these stories to the mokopuna, so they are pleased, and they think now it is a good thing that she has come back.

Too cracked now, this voice, for the singing, but Ani she wants to learn the old songs and pushes till she hears them. Together we sing them, in the night time, and her voice it is like Hana's, sweet like the tui's. The guitar, her mother's guitar, always with her – takes it to the school each morning for playing to the tamariki, and brings it back in the afternoons.

Often now the mokopuna come with her, laughing and jostling by her side, and these times I look down the hill to see them climbing the path and think that it is Hana who comes. Hana with the tāina. But those times are long ago now. Sleeps now Hana. Sleep too the tūpuna. Waits, this kuia, till she joins them; waits for Hine-Nui-Te-Pō.

Ani, she is a favourite here now. The women, they come about the children they say, but they sit on this old one's porch and talk and laugh with her for hours, knitting or weaving, with their tongues going faster than their fingers. Even Uncle Arapeta, he comes once with the letter from the tax department, and Ani it is who helps him. Hemi, he doesn't know anything about the figures, so Uncle Arapeta says, and he doesn't want that man from the department coming to see him again this year.

Favourite too with the young men, Ani. Timi Ratapu, Johnny Rewi, Para Jones – all have called since Ani came. Not to see this old one they come. But Selwyn Huata, he is the one now. Comes often, Selwyn, riding up this hill on the motorbike, and together they go, she on the back wearing the hard hat he brings for her. Worry then I, till they come back. Always I worry for her.

Sitting now, this old one, on the porch, looking down the hill. Sitting, waiting for their return. A picnic today, said Ani, and packed much kai into a kit for the two of them. Came Selwyn for her early, and they went. Kissed this cheek, Ani, before they left, then away down the hill to the motorbike. To Waimahana they go today.

"Do you know Waimahana Bay, Nanny?"

"Āe, e Ani, āe. Lived there, the tūpuna, in the old days. Good times those, in Waimahana. Before they sold the land."

Sitting now, thinking of Waimahana. On the floor, the threads of the tāniko waiting to be woven. But idle these old hands today. Waiting...

Then she comes. The ancient one. Walks she, up the hill, and stand I to meet her. But stops she by the gate, and these old eyes strain to see.

Auē. Take this old one, e Hine. Take not the young again. Turns she, and looks along the coast. Not to Waimahana, e Hine, your work is here today.

Turns back then, she, and comes toward the house.

* * * * * * *

Flax kit swinging distractedly, she comes, hurrying up the hill in the late afternoon sun.

"Nanny, I'm home. Oh Nanny, I hope you weren't worried. We had an accident, Nan, with the motorbike – it's a miracle we weren't killed. But we're all right. Nanny, are you asleep? Nanny..."

She crouches by the chair, fingers feeling around the wrinkled wrist, head to the heart, listening. For a long time she stays, then raises herself to stand near the front of the veranda, hand resting on the outer rail, facing down the hill toward the settlement. To her right the white sand continues in its curving sweep around the bay, and on it children play at running and digging, while older ones wade in the surf. A large black dog races along the beach putting a group of scavenging gulls to screaming flight. High above, a solitary plane inches its way across the sky, heading southward toward the city.

Further up the hill, behind the house, rest the tūpuna, guarded by a paling fence with white paint peeling.

Soon, in response to her call, the people will be coming. Who then will give the karanga?

"E Kui – I will do the calling." Slowly she steps down from the veranda and walks to the kawakawa by the gate, snapping a small branch to fashion for her hair.

"Hāere mai ra i te ahuatanga o to tatau aitua e...e...e!
Hāere mai, hāere mai ra!"

Te Matakite was shortlisted for The Katherine Mansfield Memorial Award 1977; and broadcast on *Radio New Zealand*, first in 1978.

1900s mid decades

Following the two World Wars, in the mid decades of the 1900s, New Zealand society was largely still rural and small-town based. Though there was increasing movement to urban living as the population rose to 2 million, then to 3 million just 20 years later, most New Zealanders still identified strongly with the land. The national economy was farming-based, with a popular image of Kiwi manhood being the 'good keen man' – one who avoided towns, preferring to live as a farmworker or hunter in remote areas.

An allied concept, though applying to the population more generally, refers to that indispensable farming commodity, number 8 wire. Originally referring to the gauge of wire (0.16inch, or 4.06mm diameter) used to build fences, it came to embrace a much wider context due to a Kiwi ability to construct, adapt, fix any manner of items using whatever resources were at hand – often made necessary by the physical isolation of these islands in the South Pacific. The term became a metaphor for what is proudly regarded as a national character of capability, ingenuity, and inventiveness, a let's-get-the-job-done attitude that has resulted in New Zealanders producing a long list of inventions and 'firsts'.

Life was generally comfortable for the majority of the European or Pākehā population. From the beginning of their shared history there had been intermarriage between the races, but a century on from the signing of the Treaty of Waitangi in 1840 those who identified themselves as Māori had not enjoyed an equal measure of prosperity, leading to some dissatisfaction.

The New Zealand Regiment was deployed in Malaya, and a

force was sent to the Korean War. By the later '60s, however, there was increasing protest and civil action against this country's involvement in the Vietnam War.

New Zealanders continued to make their mark in sporting and other areas of international prowess.

THE RAPE OF FARLEY'S GARDEN

Even allowing for the maturity and compassion I must have accrued over all the years since the event, I still find it difficult to feel sorry for Farley.

Farley Turnbull was one of those boys who every other kid hates. It wasn't that he was extra-rough, or rude, or even downright dumb – he wasn't. That was the trouble. All that time ago in Wairata, Farley didn't fit in.

Even his name wasn't right. At that time in Wairata boys were called John. Or Ted. Toms, Bills, and Henrys were okay too, and even my Hamish was permitted because it was an old family name. But Farley was another thing. Perhaps if Farley had been called John or Ted, it might have worked out. But I doubt it. Too many odds were stacked against him.

Farley was good mannered, polite, and well spoken. I think he was the only boy in Wairata who never had to write out a hundred lines correcting the phrases 'I seen him' and 'I done it'. And, as though that wasn't enough of a handicap, Farley was bright. None of us really minded that the class's average mark was regularly topped by at least 35 points in spelling or social studies. But Farley was a boy who, having gained a score of 97 per cent in arithmetic, would go up and ask the teacher to explain where he had gone wrong.

And that's what was hard to take. You just didn't do that sort of thing then.

I'm not even sure that Farley's own family quite understood

him either. Mr Turnbull was a machinery operator out at the quarry, like many of the other men in the town, and I find it hard to believe that his son's extra quota of intelligence and application had its beginnings from that source.

Mrs Turnbull was a mousey sort of woman – quietly spoken, far from an outward gregarious type either. I've wondered since, if sheltering behind that faded facade was in fact a frustrated and unfulfilled academic, with nothing greater than secretaryship of the Church Ladies' Auxiliary to extend her mental faculties.

Farley was a later child, and his two older brothers had left home before his formative years. One of them once spent a week at home when on leave from the army before being sent to serve in Malaya. Had it been my brother, or Tom's or Henry's, we'd have gone around bragging, wanting to show him off to our friends, but Farley never said a word about him. I guess they didn't have anything in common either.

In those days in Wairata, the high point of the school's cultural calendar was the annual garden contest. Almost everyone in the school entered. There were two categories in gardens – flowers and vegetables. Both were open to everyone, but an unwritten rule was understood and adhered to. In all the years I can remember, the girls grew flowers and the boys grew vegetables.

Except Farley. For years he chose to nurture sweet peas, violas, and night-scented stock in his ten-foot square plot. And for every one of those years he carried off the ten-shilling prize.

But one year, for no reason any of us could fathom, Farley switched. Maybe his father had something to do with it, or perhaps after winning the flower section for so long, he needed a challenge, but whatever prompted the change, it soon became clear that he was after the vegetable prize this year. And whereas none of the boys ever minded when he took home the honours in the girls' section, as we called it, the ten-shilling vegetable prize was contested with a keenness that eclipsed even the chance of going to the big top on the rare occasions that a circus arrived in town and set up on the domain.

Ten bob to us then was real riches, and every one of us had our own ideas on how we would use it if it came our way. I wavered between spending the lot on a good fishing rod and allowing myself sixpence a week so it would last for months. That's if I was lucky enough to get it.

Right from the start Farley's carrots and broccoli, his parsnips and beans, presented a challenge. Regular surreptitious sorties for observation purposes kept us informed of the progress of all other competitors, and while the competition between friends was good humoured, it could run high between contestants who were not so close.

Two weeks before judging day, Henry Carr, Tom Grainger, and I got together on the matter after school. We visited all the likely contenders for the title, and the money, silently viewing each plot, and making mental notes on the size and condition of every variety of vegetable.

Until we came to the last plot, things were running pretty much neck and neck, as they usually did. John Thompson's carrots had very vigorous tops, but we suspected they'd be past their best on the day. Timing was important, and gardens were planned so that everything was at its peak at the right time. Tom's beans were looking good, though I could see that Ted Logan's had him worried. There was no doubt that so far John Campbell's cucumbers were winners, but I thought to myself that my row of sweet corn at the rear of the plot was a masterstroke.

The last garden was Farley's. Rather than call in on a more formal visit, the three of us chose to peer through the hedge at it from the road. Even at a distance it was clear that the ten-bob was a goner, and although the money was normally the prime consideration, all of a sudden it didn't seem so important. Right then the main thing was the honour, and there was no way we'd relinquish that to a former flower grower. Especially if he was Farley. We returned to my place and sat on the stump of the old elm tree, hopes blighted.

Which of us was the first to mention foul play, I can't say – but I believe the idea was immaculately conceived in all three minds simultaneously. The very thought of deliberately spoiling the work of another contestant both thrilled and horrified us. Although competition had always been keen, never before had such an idea occurred to us. But then, never had the stakes seemed so high. John Thompson's carrots, Ted Logan's beans were one thing – we wouldn't have dreamed of laying a finger on them. But each luxuriant leaf, every piece of flourishing foliage in Farley's garden offended us.

Agreeing on a method wasn't so easy. Tom fancied a simple night raid about a week before judging day, but that was ruled out as being far too risky – and besides, even our consciences couldn't condone such a blatant all-out attack. No, it would have to be something more subtle. Something that preferably would never be suspected as sabotage – and even if it was, could never be pinned on us.

I did think for a moment about borrowing Uncle John's goat, but Henry pointed out that no goat could possibly pass up all the other gardens in town on its way to Farley's, then somehow open the gate and go in, without a certain amount of suspicion falling upon it. And, consequently, on us.

"What we want," said Henry, thinking aloud for all of us, "is something natural. Something…" And right then all three of us yelled the answer together and started to make a plan.

In the fortnight that followed, we resumed interest in our individual gardens. My row of corn was maturing right on schedule, and I was confident that the judge's eye would be caught by the heavy cobs, which would be ripe to perfection. My parsnips and beetroot were well up with anyone's, and if my biggest cauliflower didn't turn to seed too early, I figured I stood a fighting chance.

Tom had convinced himself that his beans were now far superior to Ted Logan's, but I thought it was just wishful thinking. Overall, though, his plot was looking good. Henry's too was a definite possibility. With several others around the town also doing well, it was going to be a good fight this year.

With two days to go, the three of us left our cultivating and concentrated on another matter. After school that afternoon and the next we went all around town, and out to Henry's grandpa's farm – each of us carrying a shoebox. By the Friday evening we were well pleased with our work, and confident that tomorrow's results would be all we hoped for.

Just one more task remained to be done, and that night it was completed. It was almost half past nine before I got home, having said at seven that I'd just run over to Tom's for a few minutes. I got a telling-off for that, but I didn't mind a bit. In another ten minutes I was in bed, grinning in the dark, thinking of tomorrow morning.

All this time later I don't remember who it was that won the prize for the best vegetable garden that year. But one thing I know – it wasn't Farley. It wasn't me either, but that didn't matter. Nor did Tom or Henry really mind that they'd missed out on the money.

I think that if any of us had such a sum we'd have willingly given it to be able to see the expression on Farley's face that Saturday morning when he found his garden stripped of its former glory. And, sleeping off the previous evening's debauchery, a hundred and eighty two of the biggest, ugliest, and hitherto hungriest snails in the whole of Wairata.

The Rape of Farley's Garden was broadcast on *Radio New Zealand*, first in 1978, published in *Bay of Plenty Times* in January 1985, and in *This Side of the World*, anthology, 2007.

A WHIMPER AND A BANG

I know what you'll think when you hear this story, and I'd like to say right at the outset that I don't blame you. I'm a practical man so I didn't believe it either to begin with. And I still wouldn't – if it weren't for the evidence.

But before I get to that, I'd better tell you just what happened.

The fire was two weeks ago come Sunday – at about two o'clock in the morning. Just about half the town turned out, all the same. Well, they do in a small place like this, where anything out of the ordinary is newsworthy – though not as much as a few years ago before we got the new telephone system.

In those days the fire siren would sound, and you'd only have to pick up the receiver to have one of the girls on the exchange tell you without your having to ask – "The fire's at Wilson's barn", or "Johnson's house in Grey Street," or whatever the case may be. Then everyone would jump on their pushbikes and race to the spot. But since we got the automatic system the exchange girls have gone and, like the children of Israel, you've got to follow the column of smoke. And not so many bother any more. Even a really good fire doesn't have the entertainment value it used to. I recall going to only a couple since I got Bruno for company, and he's four now.

This one, though, drew a good crowd – almost like the old days. Probably because of the explosion that started it. I suppose many people, like me, were woken by the sound of the bang, got up to look outside, and were drawn by the great tongues of flame that were already shooting up into the sky. From our place it didn't look far away, just across the railway line, so I decided to go and take a look.

I went to the garage to get out the old bike, my legs not being as quick as they used to be, forgetting I'd locked up after mowing the lawn, so I had to go back to the house for the key. Consequently, by the time I'd unlocked the door, clipped a torch to the front of the bike, and pedalled over the line, there was already a good crowd there.

The building that housed Thompson's Furs, Skins, and Hides was burning with an intensity approaching that of the fires of the great Day of Judgment. Or so I imagine from the graphic descriptions that remain etched in my mind from Sunday school days of more than seven decades ago.

The volunteer brigade was doing its best, but I could see there wasn't going to be much left of the building by the time they made any impression on the flames. Bill Thorn and a couple of others were propping up a ladder against the side wall – it looked as though they were planning to get a hose inside through the window above the door.

I saw my friend Monty standing watching a short distance away. I went over and asked, "Any idea how it started?"

"Gidday Dave," he said, "Not really, but there seems to have been an explosion at the beginning. Some of the chemicals they use in the tanning process, I suppose."

Bill Thorn was up at the window – I noticed it was already partially open. As he pulled it further outward to push the hose inside he dropped something. I saw it fall to the ground and went forward to pick it up and throw it back up to him. But as I stooped to retrieve it one of the other firemen asked me, and none too politely at that, to get out of the way. Couldn't blame him for forgetting the niceties, under the circumstances. I went back to stand by Monty again.

We stayed there for the best part of an hour or so, it could have been more, watching as the fire got the better of the situation. Not that there'd ever been much doubt that it would. Finally, the brigade just stood back and played the hoses around the perimeter – there wasn't much more that could be done.

Sometime during that time, I became aware of a weight pressing against my upper right leg and looked down to see Bruno beside me. He must have found his way on his own. I'd given him a whistle when I'd gone for the bike, but he hadn't responded – must have been out somewhere. He's got his own door into the garage. Well, that's to say I sawed off half a plank in the back wall and tacked a sack over the hole on the inside – so he comes and goes as he likes.

Anyway, after a while when it was obvious there was no point in staying any longer, the crowd dispersed. I rode back home over the railway line with Bruno loping along beside me.

Next day there was a picture of the burnt-out shell in the *Star*, with a rueful-looking Herb Thompson in the foreground. The write-up said it was doubtful whether the business would open up again – there's not the money in the hides trade the way there used to be, Herb was reported as saying.

Wednesday's paper carried a few inches on the front page to the effect that the police were still carrying out investigations into the cause of the blaze. It had started with an explosion all right – something in a can near a drier had gone up. The police thought it was petrol, but Herb Thompson assured them there was none of that in the place.

Apparently, a couple of men from the insurance company were in town asking questions too. Some said it didn't look good for Herb, but everyone in town stuck by him. The trouble with these out-of-towners is that they look only at situations and not people. If they knew the Thompson family as we all do, they'd know there's no way at all that Herb had anything to do with the fire.

It was around then that I first heard about what Dotty was saying. Old Dotty's had that nickname for decades now. To schoolchildren of course every teacher's old, and when the term first stuck to Miss Dorothy Morrison she was probably not much more than 35. Over the years, though, and particularly since she retired, everyone has known her as Old Dotty. The older she's got, the more it suits her – in more ways than one, some are saying now.

Can't say I blame them for that either. I must admit that when Monty told me what he'd heard, we both had a good chuckle over it too. Harmless old soul, we agreed. But when it came out that she'd been to the police station with her story, Old Dotty became a real laughing stock around the town. Well, what would *you* think about a tale like this one?

Old Dotty lives right by Thompson's Furs, Skins, and Hides, and according to her, she saw something that night that she reckons is connected with the fire.

Sometime after midnight, she says, she was woken by her cat jumping on her bed. It clawed at the bedspread and meowed repeatedly, then jumped down and stood crying at the kitchen door. Old Dotty got up, opened the door, and Sheba shot out. Dotty went back to her room and was about to get back into bed when she heard a sound outside. She peered out between the curtains, and from what she says Thompson's yard was full of animals.

There were a few farm beasts including a couple of horses,

a goat or two, but most of them were dogs and cats. And the funny thing about the sight was that there was no fighting among any of them – they were walking around and greeting each other just as though it was a proper social gathering and they all knew each other well. Even Dotty's Sheba, who can't stand the sight of a dog and won't let another cat come anywhere near the property.

Well, Old Dotty says she stood and watched for some time, and what she says followed is where her story loses credibility with everyone.

According to her, the animals seemed to be waiting around, as though they had a purpose for being there. Then a big dog turned up carrying something quite large and square-shaped in its mouth, and the others all ran to it and gathered around. She couldn't see what was happening, but there was no scrapping – it didn't look as though any of them were fighting over whatever it was.

Then one of the dogs, followed by a couple of cats, left the group and went over to the horses who were standing off a bit near the street. They stood together for a minute or two, then the group – horses, dog, and cats – came further into the yard and walked toward the factory.

Old Dotty says they seemed to know what they were doing. The two horses stood side by side close up to the building, just by the side door. Other animals arranged themselves, side-on to the horses, according to height. Then, and this is where the story gets too far-fetched for even Dotty's staunchest friends, several of the larger dogs mounted by means of the living staircase and lined themselves up side by side across the backs of the two horses.

Just so you've got that picture right in your mind, I'll go over it again. First there's the two horses standing together side by side, then on top of them, crossways, stands a row of dogs. Five, thought Dotty, though she couldn't swear to that detail.

When they were in position, up jumped another group – medium-sized dogs this time – and arranged themselves on top of the large dogs.

"Just like a circus act," Old Dotty explained it.

"I know," said Monty when someone was telling us about it for the first time, "then a cat in a pink tutu and holding a bunch of balloons jumped right on top of the lot and the horses danced in perfect precision around the yard while the rest sang *Be Kind To Your Four-footed Friends* at the top of their voices."

Well, Monty's version was more colourful than Dotty's, but not as dramatic in the long run.

What actually happened next, according to her, was that the big dog that had arrived with something in its mouth, picked it up again, climbed the animal staircase, and onto the horses' hindquarters. Once there it clambered over the two tiers of dogs until it was standing on top of the lot. Then this dog poked its nose under the frame of the partly-open window of the building, pushing it open further till it was able to scrabble up over the window-sill, still holding the large square object in its mouth. Old Dotty says it glinted when it caught the over-head light – it must have been made of metal, she concluded.

The dog dropped out of sight, she said, but appeared at the window a minute or so later. It dropped back onto the living platform, then to the ground. It no longer had anything in its mouth. The other dogs in the formation jumped down, and the pyramid reverted to its separate parts. After another short huddled conference, or so it looked to Old Dotty, the animals trooped out the gate and she couldn't see where they went because the macrocarpa hedge on the Potakas' property blocked the view.

I suppose the police recorded Dorothy Morrison's statement and thanked her politely, perhaps adding a note to the effect that the event took place at night, and she'd worn glasses for several decades. But everyone else in the town had a real field day over the sheer implausibility of the tale.

Including me, I'm sorry to say. Heaven knows, I've nothing against her, and if that's what she thinks she saw, it's not doing anyone else any harm. That's what I'm going to say to anyone I hear laughing about her in future. I'm just sorry I can't say more to defend her, but you can see the spot I'm in – if I try they'll say I'm as mad as she is.

And she's as sane as I am – I'm certain of that now. I've been sure of it ever since I went to cut the lawn this morning.

The first thing that happened was I couldn't find the petrol for the motor-mower. I keep it on a wooden box just inside the garage door – it's always there in a square can. But today it was gone, even though the door's been locked ever since I put it back there last time I mowed. I remember it was about a third full then.

I had to go down to the service station and buy a new can. That's when I put my hand in my pocket and found something I'd slipped in it last time I wore the jacket. A fortnight ago come Sunday. For a moment I couldn't think how it had got there, then I remembered the scene at Thompson's Furs, Skins, and Hides, and what I thought Bill Thorn had dropped when he was at the top of the ladder pushing the hose in the window above the side door.

Of course, I'd wondered since where Bruno's collar had got to, but didn't have any clue how he'd lost it until I found it in my pocket this morning.

As I said at the beginning, I know what you're thinking, and I don't really blame you. I'd still be just as sceptical myself if I didn't have the evidence right here in my hand.

A Whimper and a Bang was published in *New Zealand Woman's Weekly*, 26 February 1996.

OLD NICK

The cross hairs rested firmly on the forehead of his prize. Lying full-length on the grassy crown of the hill, sighting downward, the young man was calm. Although his palms were moist, the hands that held the rifle were rock-steady. They needed to be.

Three days it had taken to find them. Three days of careful tramping, keeping to the tops wherever possible. And finally, there they were, grazing in the late afternoon sun, about halfway down the valley. Some of the she-goats rested in a patch of shade, lean legs folded beneath their swollen bellies, while the younger animals cropped nearby. Among them, standing proud, was Old Nick. Unmistakable. Through the 'scope he could see the long grey beard, wary eyes, the sweeping curl of the powerful horns. The men had been right – what a head! Fourteen inches, no way. They'd have to be sixteen, maybe seventeen. They had to be.

For some time the man gazed, deliberately delaying the moment of triumph – the one he had anticipated for so long. A head shot from the .222 would split the skull, and he wanted that head intact. Better to aim for the shoulder, as long as that put the brute down till he could reach it. Too many of them got away, entrails dangling, after a misplaced gut-shot. But he had already made his choice a hundred times in his imagination. The barrel of the rifle eased downward slightly, tracing the cross hairs past the end of the straggly beard to rest on the shoulder of the beast. His forefinger tightened on the trigger.

Down in the valley Old Nick leapt then crashed down onto the grass as the bullet slammed home, its explosive force tearing through the muscle, biting deep into the bone. Moments later the sound of the sharp crack put the herd to full flight. Springing as though from a catapult they scattered across the slope, urged on by the reverberating echoes returned by the further hillsides. Then, as though on command, the company swung to the west, heading toward a narrow scrubby gully into which they all disappeared. Only Old Nick remained.

He lay, motionless, but with head high to catch the scented breeze. As the sound of the departing animals died away, he made an effort to rise. Scrabbling with the near front leg, and pushing with the rear, he pulled himself up, testing his weight on the smashed shoulder. Tentatively he tried a few steps then, satisfied, stood still, raising his nose to the wind again. The movement high on the skyline caught his eye, and in a moment he was turning and slipping away to the southeast as quickly as he could manage.

Up on the top the man swore and raised the rifle to his eye once more. For some seconds he tried to zero in on his quarry. A bullet into the other shoulder would stop him, but at that distance with a moving target, he'd have to be lucky. And at all costs he wanted that head intact. He clicked on the safety-catch, thrust an arm through the sling of the weapon and set off downhill, sliding heavily. Partway down he noticed a small ridge just in front of the moving prize. Once Old Nick passed underneath that, he'd be lost from view for a time. The man increased his pace for a few strides then, treading unevenly on a protruding clump of turf, crashed down bending one leg beneath him, then sliding some distance further on his hip.

He lay still for some seconds after the slide had stopped. He was winded, and aware of a growing pain down his left side. He rolled onto his back to view the scraped leg, and a sharp pain shot through his instep. A groan broke from his lips. Ashamed, he turned it into a furious curse. Old Nick hadn't uttered a sound. Only too often he'd heard the scream of a wounded goat downed by a shoulder or gut shot. But Old Nick had taken it in silence.

Reaching for his rifle the man scrambled to his feet, and started down again, picking his way more carefully now, conscious of the continuing pain, but determined to carry on. What was a twisted foot with such a prize at stake? The irony of his injury forced a grim smile to his lips. They were both wounded now. That evened up the chase.

Below the small ridge he could see that Old Nick had gained ground from the accident, and he pressed on after him. There was no hope trying for a hind shot – the best he could do was to keep the beast out in the open. As long as it didn't get across to the other side of the valley where the bush started. There'd be no chance of getting a shot in there. Might run into a patch of ongaonga too, and he could do without that. Get enough stings from those leaves and it'd be good-bye goat. Good-bye everything maybe – he'd heard of the nettle killing a chap before. It paralysed with its poison, so they said. So, keep him out of the bush.

He figured the two of them must be making about the same pace – the distance between them was staying fairly even. Then some three hundred yards ahead of him the animal started to climb, and the man's hopes dropped a little. Keeping up on the flat was one thing, but he couldn't be expected to climb as well as a bloody goat.

He had to admire Old Nick. There he was with a smashed

shoulder, and he was still climbing straight up that slope. Then, as he watched, the billy's near foreleg missed a hold and slipped, the damaged one collapsing under the sudden weight. The beast tumbled backward in a series of twisting jerks and lay still.

The young man hurried on, his hopes rising once more. He drew level with the spot where the animal had commenced its climb, and looked up. Old Nick was dead at last – must be. Just two hundred feet up and the head would be his. All he had to do was pack it back to the homestead and his name would be made. He could just see the look on the men's faces when he walked in tonight with his prize.

The throbbing in his foot was worse now, aggravated by the hurrying of the last few minutes. His boot felt tight, and the swelling seemed to increase by the moment. The man sank onto the grass and leaned back against the hill. Five minutes rest and he'd go on up.

It was a slight scrambling noise that warned him, and a moment later a small clod of earth bounced down the hill to rest beside the rifle. He twisted around to see a sight that stunned him. Old Nick was on the move and making again for the top. With a few more bounds the animal reached his goal and disappeared over the crest.

Flinging himself at his rifle, the young man let go a hasty shot toward the summit. He knew it was too late, but a wild fury urged him to follow it with a second. The shots seemed to roll around the small valley, returning to mock him from every direction. With renewed determination he started to climb.

At the point where Old Nick had lain there was fresh blood on the ground, and twice during the upper part of the climb he saw a drop or two still clinging to a blade of grass. At the top he paused, his breathing audible, and looked around. For almost a full minute he saw no sign of his quarry, then he picked out the moving spot, tail on and well down toward a flat ridge he'd walked up that morning on his search. Old Nick had made good time downhill. Ignoring the protesting foot, the young man started after him.

With his back to the lowering sun, the shadow before him was grotesquely long – a thin and irregular spectre leading him down the slope. He glanced at his watch and estimated there was only forty minutes left before the diminishing light would force him to abandon the hunt. He was a good walk from where he left his horse – he'd have to manage that in the half-light. No worries from there on. That horse knew every bit of the station between here and the homestead. Which was more than he did.

It seemed he was gaining again. He made careful note of the distance between himself and Old Nick when he reached the flat ground of the ridge, and within a short time of following could swear that it was lessening every minute. If he could keep up the pace he'd be right. The prize would still go home tonight as he had promised.

The goat was definitely failing. The man was wondering whether he should risk another pot-shot in the hopes of ending the chase sooner, when he noticed the animal stumble then recover several times within a short space. Once it stopped, then began again in a different direction, and the hunter adjusted his line to follow, gaining by the moment.

The next move was sudden. One second Old Nick was in view, a distance in front, and the next he gave a few quick steps to the right and disappeared over the side of the ridge. Keeping his eye on the place where the goat had disappeared, the man ran to the spot, following recklessly in the failing light. He was close now. A short distance ahead he could hear the sound of Old Nick moving and breathing heavily with the effort, but they were in deep shadow and short scrub covered the uneven sides of the sharp gully into which they'd dropped.

He took the rifle from his shoulder and moved forward, his breathing quickening. The shaded area held the chill of dusk, but he was unaware of the prickly sensation on his bare arms and legs. The excitement of the anticipated kill urged him on. Downward they went – the goat slipping through the ferns and undergrowth, the hunter brushing it aside impatiently, heedlessly. Closer, closer... The foliage was about his face now, but the chase was almost over.

In another instant the two broke through into a small clearing on a piece of level ground only metres square. Old Nick stopped in his flight and turned to face his pursuer. For many long seconds he stood, worn out from the running and the loss of blood. When the final stroke came he seemed to fold the forelegs beneath him, and collapse onto the waiting ground.

For a long time the man stood in the small bush clearing, gazing at the still body before him, then in growing realization at the vegetation that surrounded them, with the mass of serrated leaves among the fern. Old Nick was clever all right. Hunter and hunted they had been, but they would be victors together.

He was aware now of the tingling chill as it crept across his body, and began to rub his arms and legs.

He fancied he could feel the numbness already.

Old Nick was broadcast by Radio New Zealand first in 1978 and published in *The Bay of Plenty Times,* September 1985.

MYRA

The gate banged hard behind her as Myra stepped onto the footpath. A jarring bang. Not the clean click of a catch being caught and held, but the thudding sound of metal hitting warped wood and bouncing back.

It had been like that for some time now, but Myra no longer noticed it. It didn't matter anyway, now all the children were finally at school and the necessity for having them inside the barrier had lapsed. Not that the low fence had ever proved more than a few moments handicap to any of her five. Even the smallest limbs soon learned the art of climbing up the netting and swinging over to the freedom of the street.

She started along the path with care, her right arm clasped across her body, attempting to contain the hurt. If she didn't overdo it, she should make it to the end of the following block before the pain forced her to stop.

There was a bench seat there, provided years ago for the comfort of the pensioners from the council flats as they waited for the bus. A few months after it had been erected the routes had changed and now no bus came within three blocks of it. But the seat had remained, to be used occasionally by elderly walkers and more often by the children of the street as an aid in their games.

Myra walked with her eyes fixed on the distant bench. She was now at the end of the first block. Step down from the pavement … cross the road … step up. The constant ache intensified as she mounted the far pavement. The arm across her waist gripped more tightly as she forced herself toward her goal. Thank God the street was all but deserted. No one saw her lean her weight on the scarred wood back then lower herself onto the seat.

For almost ten minutes she rested. The throbbing in her side eased and she wondered which way she should go now. If she continued straight ahead and climbed the hill, the walk would be shorter. But could she manage the hill? If she turned to the left the journey would be two blocks further. But no hill. Normally the rise was no problem and Myra preferred the climb to the extra distance, but today was different.

"Hello Myra. Gathering strength for the climb?" the voice from behind startled her, and she almost cried out from the knife that stabbed through her body as she jerked. Hell! June Slagg. Of all people. What's she doing home from work today?

"Hello June." She answered without turning her head fully, hoping it was just a passing remark as the other woman strode by, but she had stopped and turned around to face her.

"Good God! Look at you. He sure did you over this time, didn't he."

Myra tried to turn her face away, but it was too late.

"What do you mean?" she started to say. As she spoke the broken tooth caught on her lip.

"C'mon dear, you didn't get that face out of a beauty salon. Hell's bells, why do you stay with him? I told you last time, didn't I? Get up and go."

Myra shrugged. She dropped her hand into her lap. There was no point trying to hide her battered appearance.

"Where to?" She didn't expect an answer. There wasn't one. Not an easy one, anyway.

"Anywhere. Just go. Surely you've got somewhere…"

"There's the children."

"Yeah, the children. That's tough. I'm glad I didn't have that problem to worry about. Just got up and went, didn't I. Left him to his booze and his birds and walked out. Best thing I ever did. When there's kids it's tough. Damn glad I had more sense than that." Her tone softened. "Look Myra, is there anything I can do?"

Myra sat, her eyes on the grey hardness of the concrete path. June waited, then sighed.

"No? Then I'd better be going." She hesitated, then added, "Well, if there is anything…" and strode off.

That's the last thing Myra needed – June Slagg butting her nose in. As it was, no good would come of their meeting, that was for sure. The news would be all around the neighbourhood after tonight's session down at the tavern. Well, what the hell – everyone probably knew already. There's not much you can keep quiet in this sort of area. Too many June Slaggs around.

Myra watched the tall figure begin to climb the hill, then raised herself from the wooden bench and turned to the left.

The ache in her side grew stronger again as she walked the first block. It was certainly worse than yesterday. Lucky it was Monday and the kids were back at school. She had hidden the pain from them yesterday, so she thought, but knew she couldn't have kept up the pretence today. Then there was tomorrow, and the rest of the week to come.

Strange that none of them had mentioned her face. No, not strange at all. Of course they'd known. They'd seen it happen before, hadn't they. Probably woke up with the noise on Saturday night. Well, she shook her head at her stupidity, it was her own fault. You'd think I'd bloody learn, wouldn't you, she asked herself as she waited for a car to pass before crossing the next street.

He'd come in happy, though belligerent, flourishing two bottles, offering one to her.

"Well, if it ain't Santa Claus," she'd greeted him, "pissed as a skunk." Like she said, it was her own fault.

A woman was coming down the footpath toward her. She was carrying two string bags laden with groceries. Some steps away she stopped to put them down, rubbing the fingers of each hand where the plaited handles had cut into them. She looked at Myra's face as the other reached her, then stooped, picked up the bags again and hurried on.

June was right, of course. She had to do something this time. If she couldn't leave, then he'd have to go. She'd charge him. That's what she'd do. Right after she'd been to the doctor, she'd call in at the police station and ask them to pick him up. She was mad to have let him get away with it before. This time he'd be sorry. This time he'd be made to pay.

There'd be the visit to the police station though – she didn't look forward to that. Not after the last couple of times. They don't like it when you refuse to lay a charge after all – she'd done that twice now, hoping the scare would be enough to change things.

The police didn't like it, but she was the one who had to live with him, wasn't she. So this time she'd go through with it – for the kids' sake as well as her own. More than her own. It did them no good to see it happen. She'd go to the police station. After the doctor.

Only a block to go, but the worst part of the walk. Past the shops, and even at this time on Monday morning she was bound to meet someone she knew. The dairy, the butcher, the

– hell and dammit, there was the vicar's wife coming out of the bookshop. Myra turned to gaze unseeing into the window beside her. That was lucky – the other woman had gone straight to her car without seeing her.

Myra hurried on as fast as the pain would allow. Once past the shops she'd be almost there. In her haste, the toe of her shoe stubbed an uneven paving stone and she was pitched forward onto hands and knees. Knives stabbed and stabbed again, and at last great sobs engulfed her. She heard hurrying footsteps behind her and somehow, God knows how, found the strength to push herself to her feet and stagger on.

Almost there. Up the path. Now push down on the door handle. Inside. Myra fell back against the door, gasping for breath, one arm still clasped around her body. Well, she'd always said you'd have to be half dead before you got prompt attention here. Myra glimpsed faces staring at her from the waiting room as she was helped along to the surgery by a blue-clad nurse.

"Hello, doctor," she managed a small smile as she greeted him. "Had another accident."

His eyes took in her injuries as came toward her.

"This is no accident, Myra," he said, his eyebrows pressing together as he came to her. "I hope you're going to charge him this time."

Myra gazed at a point beyond his left shoulder.

"I dunno what you mean, Doctor. Fell down them back stairs again, didn't I?"

Myra was published in *Thursday* magazine, 8 March 1976

PINK FOR THE MASTER

A marble cake, this. That's what it's going to be. Because Danny is nine, and nine is just the right age for marble cake.

Like the one twenty-eight years ago. Made by the mother of the girl with the birthday, that one too. Eeeii, the name has gone. Not the marble cake, though. That's been remembered. For twenty-eight years. Or something.

Like magic it was, that first time. The cake sitting there, in the middle of the table. Nine candles on top of snow-white icing. Then all of them lit, and the girls singing Happy Birthday dear... dear... The name has gone. It doesn't matter – not really. It's the cake that's the real thing now.

At least, real when you're still nine. Or about.

All that white icing, covering not only the top, but all around the sides too. But when the knife cut through and a slice fell onto the plate, there were the colours. Not one, as expected, but three. And the mother of the girl laughing at the surprised faces.

A marble cake she said it was called – and the word marble rolling round and round in mind and mouth for the rest of the day and night. Marble, marvel... marble, marvel... Marvel didn't roll about on the tongue the way the other did, but it sparkled. The two together, once united, could not be separated, and stayed joined, always.

Like the colours – pink, brown, yellow. Favourites ever since, those colours. Together, that is. A floral dress that no one else ever liked, chosen because of those colours. And a beach umbrella – still in the shed out the back, a bit tatty now to use, but held onto, not thrown out. Neapolitan ice cream, with its pink, brown, white – near enough to still conjure up the magic feeling from that time, and still bought for that reason.

A good mixture, this. Just the right feel as it's stirred around the bowl. Divide it into three. Then it's time for the magic, with the two little bottles and the packet lined up on the bench.

Pink for the master. The small bottle with the bright red liquid – three drops, and mix it in. The colour a little bit orange at first, then turning bright pink as all the magic works its way through.

Who will it be who marvels this time? Which of the seven nine-year olds will sit there, mouth and eyes like a hāpuka, staring at the three colours swirling.

Jason and Justin – they've probably seen such a thing before. Jason's mother, though, she looks as though she's never eaten a cake in her life. So thin, and her son looking as though he'll end up the same way too. A nice house, theirs, around in Kotuku Drive. Danny says that the lounge suite seems to fit into the wall, instead of just sitting against it as most do. Jason's father, he's involved in the Jaycees, and a couple of times he's come to the door selling fertilizer. Or something.

Justin – he has a nice house too, though Danny says it isn't as flash inside as it looks outside. Not as good as ours even, he reckons, because the carpet doesn't come right up to the walls and there's boards showing around the edges of the rooms. But Danny likes to go home with Justin after school because there's always something left out to eat. Justin's mother doesn't get home from work till nearly five. Often the two boys, or even more, stop off there first, then come on back with Danny, crumbs around their mouths or munching at an apple. Justin doesn't have a father – not at home anyway. The story is he's gone back to England, but Justin doesn't seem to know much about it. Or care.

No, marble cake won't be anything special to those two. Nice enough little boys, both of them. And polite. But it's unlikely that three colours in one cake will seem like magic to them.

Brown for the dame. The packet this time, and two big spoons of the cocoa powder, folded into the second bowl till the mixture turns a rich chocolate colour right through. What with the bit of extra powder, the brown parts are always just that much heavier, a bit more substantial. A spoonful of milk will even them up – make it all the same. But the difference, that's good, it adds a bit of variety. Makes the chocolate parts stand out. Those are the bits that don't melt away quite so quickly in the mouth. The best parts, to be savoured more.

Paul, and Api, and Ricky – real clowns, that group. Them and Danny. Funny as a fight, that four. And their fighting funny too, sometimes. Like the time when Api took Ricky's bike home so they thought it was stolen. Then when Ricky's father phoned the police, bringing it back, so that the policeman coming out of the house saw it standing there, propped against the patrol car.

And how Ricky and his old man got their own back by taking Api's bike, so they thought, from behind his house one night – taking the frame apart and hoisting it into the Judas tree on the grass outside the place. Then bolting it back together around a couple of branches. Eeeii, that was funny. Especially when it turned out to be Paul's bike after all, and Paul's father already owed Ricky's dad one for the time they took a load of stuff to the dump and George drove off leaving his friend standing there in the middle of the boxes and bottles, yelling at him to stop. Never a dull moment around here.

And the boys, like their fathers, the best of friends underneath it all. That four! Look, they'll say – something's wrong with your cake, Danny. It's got spots – it must be sick. And, hey look at those patchy brown and yellow bits – it looks just like that little dog that lives across the road from Api's. You know the one. Hey, Mrs Henry, did you make this cake out of Parker's dog? Gee, I'm not having any of that. But wolfing it down anyway when it's handed to them. And then wanting more.

Yellow for the little boy who lives down the lane. The other little bottle, and just one drop this time. The mixture already pretty yellow from the butter and the eggs – but one more drop to brighten it up.

Peter, the last of the nine year olds, and different again. He's quieter, Peter, and more polite than the others. That's when he's with grown-ups, anyway. Out in the back yard or down the street with the others, no doubt just as much one of them. Clever, Danny says, always the one to know all the answers at school, Peter and a couple of the girls in the class. Gets that from his father probably. A lawyer out on his own, but not doing that well by the look of it. A hard-working family, Peter's. His grandfather, always in the market garden in the spare two sections alongside the house – a small man, bent right over from the years of planting and weeding. And the mother – all day in the fruit and vegetable shop serving, with the little girl sitting there playing, or helping to sweep the floor with a tiny broom.

Three bowls full. One pink, one brown, one yellow. And after all, perhaps no one will care. Or even notice.

Not the same now, these nine year olds. Not like they used to be back then. In that time there was still room for magic – for people to believe in what wasn't really there. Not anymore. Heat shields around space ships, light swords, computerized cars that talk and drive themselves and leap over cliffs – all that, yes, because that may yet come about.

And what is a three-coloured cake to all that?

Mix them all together, perhaps, in one bowl. The pink, the brown, the yellow. All stirred up well, so no one will know what it was going to be. Make it just one colour – plain khaki all through.

No. Let them stay. It's what this cake should be. Marble, marvel.

Big spoonfuls of each, into the tin – and that same small thrill at seeing the colours together. Pink, brown, yellow. Side by side. Yellow, brown, pink. Under and over. Brown, yellow, pink.

Then the best part. Using a fork now – running it through the mixture to produce those swirling patterns. To make the marble effect. The rainbow. Not to be overdone. Just enough so that the colours bend and curl into each other, creating variety. Too much and there'll be no difference between them, and no interest. But enough to blend the three into a harmony. That's where the magic lies.

Now into the oven. Forty minutes to carry on with the other preparations, to decorate the room, have a cup of coffee. The mess will wait – there'll be more to come before it's all over. Time to go down the road to the grocer, and to the butcher for the little sausages – ordered, but left till the right day. Then home again in time to take the tin out of the heat.

Eeeii – too flat, this cake. That doesn't look right at all. Oh no, the baking powder! The tin still sitting on the bench, untouched.

Where is the magic now? So sad and flat, this rainbow. And too late to do anything about it now. Isn't it? Past the time when it could be begun again, when another start could be made.

But, maybe not too late. Make the best of it – that's what can be done now. Perhaps with a good layer of covering...

Rinse out a bowl and find the icing sugar. Pile enough icing on top and maybe it will look all right. Perhaps the boys won't notice the problem underneath. You don't see that sort of thing when you're nine. And when you're having a party.

It's only when you're older – when something like twenty-eight extra years have shown you that there isn't any magic there at all. Because you've lived too many years when it hasn't been a party.

Pile on the icing. Who knows – perhaps those kids haven't seen a marble cake before. Maybe they'll still marvel over its mixture of colours and not notice its flatness. Even one of them. They haven't lived those extra years. Not yet.

And so they might see the rainbow. Because you can still believe in marble cake when you're nine. Or about.

Pink For the Master gained second place in NZWWS short story competition, 1987.

RIGHT NEIGHBOURLY

The moment we rounded the corner and spotted the unfamiliar car taking up the space where we always park the ute at this hour on a Friday, I could see Randy thinking. As I drove past to pull in three spaces further down, I noticed her checking it out with the corner of her eye.

Stickers on the back windscreen and bumper identified it as a rental. One of Avis' top of the line by the look of it. I knew what she was thinking – I should do, we've been married for coming up thirty years – and beat her to it just as she began to open her mouth.

"Bet you five bucks old Dave's got 'em nabbed already."

"Swine," she laughed, "the first round's yours."

I paused to glance in the window as we walked back past. A large fawn hat occupied the front passenger seat. Things were looking better and better.

"With a bit of luck," I said, "it'll be the only one we need worry about."

At the bar Jack greeted us in the manner he usually did – "Hi Pete, you old reprobate. Miranda – don't tell me you're still with him." Then he gave us a wink and said, with a slight jerk of his head in the direction of where we could see Dave sitting with a well-built stranger, "We'll be in for a good session tonight, I shouldn't wonder."

"Have they been at it long?" asked Randy.

"Nope. Just warming up, I should think," replied Jack, "I don't think he's up to the mozzie-copters yet."

We picked up our drinks and walked over, pausing behind the stranger's back to catch old Dave's eye. In Dave's case that's spot on the truth. He's got only one of them, and that's not too good with the details, so it sometimes takes a moment or two.

"Hey, come and join us," he called out. "Here're two friends of mine I'd like you to meet," he said to his companion.

The large man rose and shook my hand with a grip that would've been appropriate if he'd been grasping a pair of wire-cutters on a fencing job. He clenched Randy's hardly less forcibly, judging by the look that passed over her face, as Dave said, "Miranda and Pete, this is Hiram, honouring us with a visit from the U S of A."

"Pleased to meet you, Hiram," I said, "there's not much left in your glass. I'll get it filled up for you while I'm on my feet."

When I got back and sat down Randy was saying, "It'll be a good property when we've got it licked into shape. About half a dozen more years of hard work ahead I'd say, then we'll be able to start building a house." Ah, so she was giving him the full treatment.

I put down the glass in front of the visitor and was told that was right neighbourly of me.

"Pete," said Randy, "Hiram's from Texas. He's an investigative journalist. He's got a column syndicated in fifteen states." It was no wonder she'd given him the 'A' line, I thought, noting as I did so that Dave's eye was glittering. No doubt he was thinking it was jackpot week.

Hiram took a mouthful from his glass then leant back in his chair.

"Dave here," he said, looking at Randy and me, "was telling me you've got some giant-sized mosquitoes to watch out for in these parts."

"Oh sure," I said, as though it was nothing worth talking about, and Randy added something to the effect that she bet there were some pretty large ones back in Texas where he came from too. Hiram said he was pretty darn tootin' they didn't have anything that size, or that clever for that matter.

We knew our cue. Randy looked at Dave and asked, a trace of accusation in her voice, "You told him about the tourist hut then?"

"Aw heck, no," said Dave, "just about the tent. You know, the one with that honeymoon couple at the top of the lake."

"Oh, right," I chipped in, priding myself that I'd injected just the right tone of relief into my voice.

Hiram leaned forward. "There's more?" he asked.

Dave looked down at the table and shook his head.

"Nah," he said, "not a thing."

"You're quite sure?" asked the big Texan.

Dave picked up his glass, tossed off the inch or so left, then announced, "Yep, there's not a thing in it."

Hiram reached out, picked up the glass, then the other three on the table. "My turn," he stated, and made his way over to the bar. When the full ones were in front of each of us he lifted his in salute and while we were taking the first swallow said, "So, this tourist cabin, was it? Don't tell me those mozzies got underneath that and lifted it right up too."

We all snorted.

"Nah, of course not," said Dave.

"No, they couldn't do that," said Randy, "not that hut. That one's a twelve-bedder."

"And not since they tied it to the trees with wire cables," I put in.

"So they didn't get the cabin?" asked the Texan.

"No," said Randy and I almost in unison.

"Not the cabin itself," said Dave.

"What, then?"

"Well, there was this other building, you see," said old Dave, "a smaller one..."

"Another cabin?"

"No," I said, "a much smaller thing, away from the hut a bit, in the trees..."

"Oh, I see what you mean," said the Texan, "it was an outhouse. Beg your pardon, Ma'am," he added, looking at Randy.

"A dunny," she stated.

There was a half-minute silence while Hiram thought about it. The rest of us put the time to good use by taking another mouthful.

"Are you telling me they took off with the, that building? Now that would be inconvenient." Hiram let out a Texas-sized guffaw as he picked up his own joke. "A real in-convenience."

Randy put on her slightly-offended-bordering-on-pissed-off look. It's something she's perfected over the years. "Especially for the person in it," she said in the tone I associate with the one she uses when I try to get out of taking my turn at doing the dishes once a week.

"There was someone in the outhouse at the time? Don't tell me the mozzies picked it up and carried it off with someone in it!"

"There were several thousand of them," I explained, "and the man wasn't nearly as big as you are."

The Texan whistled through his teeth. "All the same," he said, "that's a pretty tall order."

Randy gave him a serious look. "I think it's best," she said, "if you think of what we've told you as a pretty tall story."

"You mean it's not true?" he asked. "I guess you've been pulling my leg all along."

"It's best you think that," repeated Randy, and Dave and I nodded our heads and agreed.

Hiram took a few sips while he thought. "I suppose," he said, "if people thought there was any truth in it, they'd be pretty scared, right?"

Randy nodded. "Especially overseas tourists," she said. "If they heard anything like that, they wouldn't come this way. I mean, think of it, we've got a good name with Japanese visitors, and they wouldn't venture anywhere near the place."

We all swilled down the dregs. Hiram reached out and collected the glasses again, leaning forward and dropping his voice.

"Just supposing such a thing could happen, how do you think the person concerned would get on? I mean, would they be found?"

Dave nodded. "Oh yeah, eventually."

"In about four days," I said.

"Four and a half," said Dave.

"That's with a big search party," I added, "forty-two men."

"Persons," corrected Randy.

"Plus back-up," agreed Dave.

"And would he be okay?"

The three of us shook our heads.

"I shouldn't think so," said Randy, "I'd say such an experience would make you mad."

"Stark raving loony, no doubt about it," said Dave, looking at the table and shaking his head.

Jack left the bar and walked over to clear some glasses from a table nearby.

"Dinner's on," he announced, "any of you staying?"

Old Dave put his hand in his pocket and jingled a few coins. Randy looked up and said, "It'd be nice, Jack, but we can't stretch to it tonight, I'm afraid."

Hiram slapped his palm down on the Formica, "Why don't the three of you stay as my guests?" he suggested.

Randy said something about not wishing to impose on his generosity, but her words were cut off as the large Texan pulled out an appropriately proportioned wallet and made the order. Jack scooped up the empty glasses and suggested that since it would take a little while to get them served, we'd have time for another round of drinks while we waited.

"Sorry, mate," said Jack some time later as he cleared away old Dave's plate, "had to be beef. No moa on the menu tonight. I can't seem to get them these days."

Dave scowled up at him, but brightened as Jack replaced his glass with a full one.

"Mowars, huh," said our visitor, "didn't I read in one of the brochures about those? Giant birds, right? Huge. I thought they were extinct."

"They are," Randy assured him, "Jack's just being funny."

"So there used to be some of them around these parts?"

"Sure," she replied in a disinterested sort of way. It's another of the many tones she's developed and got down pat.

"Used to be that this area was over-run with them," I put in. At least that's what they say. Of course, my family's only been here since 1869 so I wouldn't know, myself. Not like Dave."

"That's right," Dave said with that unfocussed and distant look he's been working on for a while now. I reckon having just the one working eye gives him an advantage. "My great-grandfather came here around 1810. Shipped out from England as a lad on a whaler. When he got here he decided to clear a little land and try his hand at settling. So he jumped ship. Guess he did all right at it, because we're still here."

"And the mowars, they were still around in your grand-daddy's day?" asked Hiram.

Dave shifted a bit in his chair and gazed off toward the bar. After a few moments of silence, during which he looked more and more uncomfortable, Randy answered for him.

"Jeez, no," she said, "the moas were gone well before any Europeans came."

The big Texan leaned forward and caught Dave's eye. I could see he was the sort of man who didn't miss much.

"Is that right Dave? What do you think? Do you go along with that?"

I helped out with an answer. "That's what the books say."

"Yeh, that's what the books say," repeated Dave. He raised his drink and took a long swallow, his eyebrows lifting ever so slightly above the rim of the glass as his eye met mine.

"And you go along with that, do you?" asked the Texan again.

"Can't argue with the books," said Dave.

Hiram waited a moment or two. I had to admit his interviewing technique was up with the best. His timing was spot on.

"So your grand-daddy wouldn't have seen any of these birds himself, then? What a shame. Why, that would really be something to talk about."

Old Dave reached his hand down into his left pocket and pulled out a smooth stone. After sweeping his coat-sleeve across the table to wipe away a couple of wet rings, he placed it down in front of him almost reverently. "He got this, though," he said, with a touch of awe in his voice. Dave looked up at the visitor and asked, "You do know what it is, don't you?"

"Well, er, can't say that I do, offhand. Other than it's a pebble."

Dave gave him a look and made as if to put it back in his pocket. "That's more than any old pebble."

"It's a moa's gizzard-stone," I said.

"Is that so?" Hiram reached across the table, but Dave was quick to cup his hand over it, hiding it from view.

"Dave, that's not *the* stone, is it?" asked Randy.

Dave said nothing. He sat there with his hand clasped tightly. Randy lowered her voice. "You didn't bring that one out with you?"

Once again I had to admire the Texan. I had no doubt he'd unearthed some good stories in his time. With his eyes right on Dave he asked, "And how did your grand-daddy know it wasn't just any old stone? It sure looks like a regular river stone to me."

An indignant look flashed across Dave's face. "You tell him, it's real," he said, appealing to Randy and me.

Randy replied with just the right level of composure mixed with concern. "It's real enough. Now put it away Dave."

Dave kept his hand clasped, a stubborn look on his face.

"You sure there weren't any of them mowars around still in your granddaddy's time?" asked Hiram.

"I'm not saying there was," answered Dave.

"Nor that there wasn't, as far as I see it," countered the Texan. "Yet it seems to me that if a man's ancestor did actually see one, that'd be really something, right?"

"That depends," said Dave.

"On what?"

"On what that ancestor did to just what moa." Old Dave's voice was low. He looked down at his balled hand.

"So, if there were only a few left..." ventured Hiram, "maybe even the very last one..." he gasped as Dave flashed Randy and me a stricken look.

The sound of a chair scraping the wooden floor broke the silence as Hiram pushed himself back from the table then scooped up all four glasses. When he returned from the bar, Dave was sitting with his head in his hands. The stone lay on the table in front of him.

"Do you mind?" asked Hiram, his hand reaching out for the stone as the three of us lifted our drinks. He rolled it around in his palm, pulling out a pair of spectacles to help him examine it at close quarters.

"So, this is the very last gizzard-stone of the very last mowar on earth," he announced.

"One of them," said Dave in a tone that admitted defeat.

"One of them?" repeated Hiram. "You mean it wasn't the very last mowar. There were more of them?"

"It was the last moa all right," replied Dave. He seemed to be in despair.

"One of its gizzard-stones," I explained, "they kept several in their crop."

"Then, you've got more of these?" The Texan's interest was keen.

"There was a handful of them originally," said Dave. He didn't seem interested in anything but his glass, but at least his depression was lifting a little. "The others were spread out around the family a generation or two ago. They've probably all been lost. I've got only that left now."

"Oh!" Hiram seemed a little let down.

"That and another one."

"Oh?"

Four glasses went up to four sets of lip, each set of eyes

focusing no further than the liquid within. Hiram put his down first. "I don't suppose you'd ever part with it." It was more of a statement than a question.

Old Dave shook his head. He didn't seem to want to talk, so I put my thoughts into words.

"I suppose it would be worth a lot. I mean if it got around what it is. But that's out of the question, of course."

Randy put her hand on Dave's.

"Quite out of the question. It's brought you nothing but embarrassment already, hasn't it?"

"Bloody moa," exploded Dave, "a bloody albatross more likely. I reckon it's been the cause of a lot of bad luck in our family over the years."

"Now Dave," said Randy, patting his hand.

"I've a good mind to throw it away for once and for all. That and the other one."

"Hold on a minute," I butted in. "One of them at least should go to the National Museum. That's when you've gone, of course."

"I reckon there's a curse on them," said Dave, looking like both his gumboots were stuck in the mud and the stream was rising. "If I sent them both off now to that museum maybe things would come right."

"You wouldn't be interested in selling them?" asked the Texan "Or even one of them?"

Dave snorted. "Who'd pay for bad luck?"

Randy and I looked at each other and stood up together.

"Time we were getting along," she announced, and began to thank Hiram for the drinks and the meal. He seemed to have something else on his mind and wasn't paying much attention to us, so we left the two of them to it.

At the door we stopped and looked back. Old Dave and the big Texan were leaning over the table deep in conversation.

"Now doesn't that look neighbourly!" I said.

"Right neighbourly," agreed Randy.

573 TO AUCKLAND

From the time of boarding, the stewardess knew she'd have reason to note seat 17E again.

The young man who thrust at her the pass bearing that number was the one she'd noticed waiting by the door of the crowded departure lounge – agitated, stubbing out one partially finished cigarette after another. For one reason, row 17 was in the non-smoking area. But there'd be more to it than that. After all these years going up and down the aisles, attending to all manner of needs, it wasn't often she was wrong.

With everyone finally seated, she moved down the left-hand side of the plane, checking seat-backs, handing out small pillows and rugs.

On the window side in row 17, an elderly couple gave her nervous smiles as she approached. She noticed their seatbelts were drawn tight, and two heavily-veined hands were clasped between them. Across the aisle, the first two seats in the centre of the cabin were occupied by a young woman and a small child. Between the boy and a large middle-aged woman in the seat on the other aisle, the young man sprawled, leaning back with eyes closed. A dark leather briefcase on his lap was clutched with both hands.

"Excuse me, sir." She had to repeat it three times before he opened his eyes. "Would you please stow your case under the seat in front and return your seat-back to the upright position in readiness for take-off."

For a long moment he sat there as though not comprehending then, with an impatient click of his tongue, he sat up and moved to comply. The stewardess waited till he had clamped the belt around his hips before she moved on.

By the time she had completed her routine the plane was starting to move. The man in 17E was hunched over his tray, writing quickly. She stopped in her stride and spoke.

"Trays must be clipped up for safety reasons," she said. "You can continue your work very shortly when we're in the air."

Once again the response was slow then, accompanied by another click of the tongue, the writing block was removed and the tray secured. She smiled at the older couple who were still clasping hands, and moved forward to take her seat at the front of the cabin.

As soon as take-off was completed and the aircraft was high above the Pacific Ocean she moved back down the aisle with an armful of comics, colouring books, and small packeted games. The woman in 17C, with her son beside her, looked as though she needed a good sleep, though it seemed unlikely she'd be getting it for some time. The stewardess handed the child a comic and a game of checkers. As the boy smiled his thanks, she noticed the man along the row open a packet of cigarettes and deliberately, it seemed, draw one out.

"This is the non-smoking area," she said, polite but firm, following her training. The cigarette went up to his mouth as he turned his head to meet her eyes.

"I specified smoking," he answered, "but there were no seats available. I was on standby." This was the first time she'd heard him speak, and the few words revealed an accent. Somewhere European, though she couldn't pin it down precisely.

"That's right. This is a full flight. If you want to smoke you can go to the rear cabin and do it there."

The man plucked the cigarette from his mouth and tapped it on the packet several times before he slid it back inside and dropped the box into a jacket pocket. The boy next to him was tearing at the cellophane wrapper of the checker set, and it gave way in a shower of red and black plastic discs. He scrabbled around, gathering them up from the seat and floor. The stewardess moved on with a smile. When she returned a few minutes later the boy had the small board set up on the tray in front of him. In the middle row one square was vacant.

"Couldn't you find them all?" she asked.

"No, there's a red one still missing," said the boy. "I looked everywhere."

"I'll see what I can do," she promised, moving away. A few moments later she was back with a game of snakes and ladders that she dropped into his lap.

They were about to begin serving the meal when a call button lit up above row 17. The mother and her son were engrossed in their game. As the stewardess reached them the mother's counter was claimed by the largest reptile on the board and the boy let out a shout of laughter. The man beside them was scowling.

"Is there some problem, sir?"

He appeared to deliberate for a moment, then spoke.

"I have been in the Pacific on assignment for my company." His words were slow, deliberate, his tone giving the impression that he was speaking to an erring child. "Two days ago I got a cable from my director telling me to go on to Auckland to take part in an important sales conference on Thursday evening. That's tonight," he pointed out, "and if I don't get this estimate prepared before I get there, I could miss out on a multi-million dollar deal."

The stewardess began to make a comment, then checked herself. It wasn't her business – her job was to make the passenger's trip as comfortable as possible. "And there's some problem?" she repeated. The man's increasing impatience was visible.

"Do I have to spell it out?" he demanded, indicating the boy with a jerk of his head. "How am I supposed to get this work done with a row like that going on beside me? You'll have to find me another seat."

There was a definite firmness in her voice as she replied. "I'm afraid every seat is full. We have begun to serve the meal, and I can't ask anyone to change with you now." She flashed a smile at the small face regarding her, the earlier smile now replaced by uncertainty. "I'm sure everyone will be quiet enough to let you get on with your work."

The boy's head nodded, and the stewardess winked at him as she took the opportunity to walk back down the aisle to the dinner trolley. They began passing out the meal trays from the rear of the cabin, and she found herself apprehensive about reaching row 17. When it came she noticed a vacant seat beside the boy. The large woman in the seat on the far aisle had already been served, and was bent over her tray, paper napkin tucked into her neckline. The stewardess handed the mother and the boy theirs, then moved on to serve the next row.

"Excuse me." Her defences rose at the tone of the voice behind her, but she turned with a smile. He smelled of smoke.

"Yes, sir?"

"What is on the menu?"

"The main course is Tournedos Clamart," she began, to be interrupted almost immediately.

"I don't normally eat red meat. I believe there's a special menu available?"

"Yes, there is," she replied, "but it must be ordered in advance. I'm sure you can appreciate that."

"It wasn't possible in my case," he followed, "I told you – I was on standby."

"There's also an entrée, vegetables, dessert, cheese and biscuits – I'm sure you'll find something to suit you. If you'd like to sit down, I'll hand you a tray."

"Hrmmph." He turned with a scowl and regarded the row of passengers. "How am I to get to my seat?"

The stewardess drew in a deep breath. In the other aisle, beside the large woman, a trolley blocked access. It was unattended – her colleague must have had to return to the galley for something. The man was clicking his tongue. She looked at the young mother.

"I'm very sorry," she apologized, "could you let this gentleman through?"

The woman picked up her tray and stepped into the aisle, while the stewardess clipped up her table. Between them, they held the boy's meal while the man squeezed through without a further word. When all were reseated she handed a tray over their heads. It was taken in silence.

With the meals all distributed, she began to serve the coffee. While she poured for the lady in 17C, the man held out his cup and she leaned across to fill that too. She noticed he had eaten all the turkey entrée and was now applying a liberal amount of pepper to the steak. A moment later a choking sneeze erupted, and the man grasped in his left-hand pocket for a handkerchief. A small red disc flew out with it, landing on his tray as he buried another sneeze in the cloth. The boy beside him retrieved the counter triumphantly.

"Look, here's my missing checker," he shouted, "he had it in his pocket all the time."

The remainder of the flight was routine, and the stewardess heard no more from the man in 17E till they landed at Auckland, when he was on his feet and waiting at the head of the cabin before the plane had rolled to a stop. The mother of the boy was one of the last to leave. She smiled wearily at the stewardess.

"I'm sorry about the problems."

"You were fine," she reassured the woman. "No bother at all. I'm sorry you had to put up with that."

The mother shrugged, then turned back as she started to step out of cabin. "You know, I rather hope he doesn't get that sales deal." The stewardess laughed.

"Don't worry. He won't." The woman looked at her, surprised.

"How can you be so sure?"

"Because he obviously doesn't know about the dateline," she answered. He said his meeting was Thursday evening. It's already Friday here in New Zealand."

<hr>

573 to Auckland was published in *Christchurch Star,* 5 January, 1979; *Bay of Plenty Times,* 19 July, 1986.

TRAVELLER

As each jandalled foot slapped down, a small flurry of brown dust scurried to make way as though each particle was escaping for its life. For almost half a mile the boy watched in bored amusement, turning around once or twice to check the flat wide footprints marching backward into the distance behind him.

On his left, toward the river, grey tattered mountains of old newsprint rose in huge regular shapes behind a wire wall. How many tons in one of those stacks, he wondered – ten thousand, a million maybe? Who knew? Or cared!

His Gran, she had saved old paper. Not that much of course, but a shed full all the same. Every piece that came into the house for years and wasn't needed to hold the kūmara peelings or other kitchen scraps destined for the chooks, or to wrap the eggs that went to Nanny Walker, was folded in four and placed in the carton in the corner of the large kitchen. When the stack grew high enough to reach above the top of the box, it was his job to carry it out to the back shed. That shed had been full when Gran went. And who cared about it then? No one had any use for a mountain of old papers. Uncle George who took over the old place needed the shed for tools and fencing wire and cleaned it all out. It took the two of them all one morning and part of the afternoon to load up the trailer and run the tractor several miles down the road to the county dump about a dozen times. And geez had Uncle George moaned.

"Why'd she want all this paper? Porangi, porangi…" he repeated through the day.

Gran had grumbled too, sometimes. About the way he dirtied his clothes, about the way he ate too much, or not enough. But he knew all along that she didn't really mean it – it was a sort of game between them, which they both understood. But with Uncle George it was different.

He tried to think what Gran would have said if she'd seen all that paper stacked by the mill. Or how many millions of eggs it would wrap. But it didn't matter now. Not anymore. The flax kete was rubbing against his leg, so he switched it over to his other hand as he walked. How far had he gone now? Two miles, perhaps three, since the last car dropped him on the other side of the town.

"We made good time," the driver had said as he slowed down to let him out at the intersection where the boy had indicated. "You'll be just in time to get to your auntie's place for afternoon tea. Good luck." Then he'd put his foot down again and was off down the main road. After a few seconds the boy followed.

He reached in the kit for the apple he knew was there, but his hand closed only on fabric. Then he remembered he'd eaten it before Opotiki, and wished he'd waited longer – till he needed it more.

He walked on past the paper mountains, trying to ignore the empty feeling. He kicked a stone along with him for a while, but once it caught his toe and pushed back the nail, hurting him. Besides, it slowed him down, and he couldn't afford to waste any more time. He picked it up and threw it as far as he could across the paddocks but didn't see it land.

It took him some moments to realize that the station wagon that had come to a stop a hundred metres ahead was waiting for him. He broke into a run and came level with it. The back of the wagon was filled with cases of books, and the driver was leaning over to open the passenger door.

"Going far?"

"To Tauranga."

"You're in luck then," said the man, "hop in."

The boy slid onto the contoured seat and placed the kit on the floor in front of him, between his feet.

"Thanks," he said.

"Pleasure," said the man, "I like a bit of company. Better do up the seat-belt – they're watching for that these days."

The boy reached behind him, and drew the grey strap across his body, fitting it into the left-hand stalk of a pair that protruded antennae-like from between the seats.

"No school today?"

"I've finished school." He tried to make his response sound slightly indignant but wasn't worried. He was big for his age and had passed before. Nevertheless, he didn't want the subject pursued. He twisted around in the seat to look at the back of the vehicle.

"You sell books?" he asked.

"That's right. I travel all over the Bay of Plenty, selling to dairies mainly. Paperbacks."

The boy didn't answer, and after a moment the man continued, "I'm based in Auckland. Away from home four nights a week, but I'll be home tonight."

"Uhuh."

"You ever been to Auckland?"

He shook his head. "Not yet."

The conversation lapsed for a while, and the boy leant back in the seat and gazed out the window. The car slowed to give way to an approaching vehicle before taking a right-hand turn, and he had time to make out the name Tauranga on the bright yellow road sign before they accelerated and left it behind in a spray of loose stones.

The coast kept them company half a mile off to their right as the car sped along, and to the left the plain stretched out almost as far as he could see. In the distance a lone peak rose from the flats, like a single sand-castle left on an expanse of otherwise unbroken beach as its builder moved on to other virgin areas. The boy kept his gaze on it, twisting his neck to follow it even as they left the sight behind.

"Mount Edgecumbe," volunteered the driver, noting his interest.

"Yeah," said the boy. Putauaki, that's what Gran called it.

"The Pākehā, they call it something else," she'd told him when telling him the stories, "but Putauaki, that's its real name."

"What's in Tauranga?" asked the man, interrupting his thoughts. For a moment the boy didn't understand and was on the defensive.

"What do you mean?" he asked, then regretted responding. He should have just kept quiet.

"Why are you going there?"

"Oh!" he relaxed a little. "My aunty – she lives there. I'm going to stay with her.

"Holiday?"

"Probably for good. I'm going to get a job." It wasn't really an untruth – he'd have to get one somewhere, wherever it was.

"Got one to go to?"

"My uncle's looking for one for me," he said. "I might go and work with him," he added, then wished he hadn't, but the man asked no more questions, and after a few silent minutes the boy leaned back again, watching as the open land gave way to more hilly country. More like home.

Then they were running right by the coast, and he could see that the familiar shingle had given way to fine sand, and he wished he could run down onto it and let its dry warmth slip between his toes the way he'd done that time he went to Mahia. The time he'd gone with Gran. Funny that it seemed so long ago, when he knew it was just last summer.

Looking out across the bay, he could scarcely see where the water ended and the sky began, except for where a distant white plume seemed to float just above where the horizon must be. It was strange to see the familiar sight from here. He felt he should have left it far behind, with the rest. But it seemed to be following him. A part of home, watching over him. He saw the driver glancing out across the blue, and forced himself to speak.

"Whakaari's smoking well today."

"Wha... oh, White Island – sure is," returned the man, and flashed him a smile. The boy was glad he'd made the effort.

They didn't speak again for some time, but it was a comfortable silence. The car was going a lot faster than the boy had been before, but he saw that the man handled it well, and he enjoyed the experience.

Sometime later the hunger pangs started again, and the boy's stomach began to growl. In embarrassment he tightened his muscles as hard as he could, but it didn't help.

"Hungry?" asked the man, after a few moments.

"No," he answered. "In fact, I'm full up. I had a big lunch in Whakatane before I left. I suppose it's just going down."

The man shot him a quick glance but resumed his watch on the road without further comment. It was some minutes later that he said casually, nodding toward the glove box.

"There's a bag of toffees in there. Get it out for me, will you?"

The boy did so, and the man took one, unwrapping it with one hand and tossing the paper into a plastic bag hanging below the parcel shelf.

"Help yourself," he invited, then added as the boy hesitated, "take a couple – I'm sure you've got room for those."

The boy unwrapped one, then sucked hard finishing it quickly. He peeled a second and tried to keep this one in his mouth longer. They helped. He screwed up the top of the cellophane bag and placed it back in the glove box.

"Thanks," he said.

In the cool comfort of the car he dropped into a sound sleep, waking only when its movement stopped. In front of them a barrier blocked the road, and two red lights flashed alternately. He sat up, and the man glanced his way.

"Just waiting for a train," he remarked. "You had a good sleep – you must have been tired."

"Yeah. I got up early this morning," the boy said. He didn't say how early.

A single engine passed in front of the car and the boy gazed with awe at the huge machine. He'd never seen one that close before. Then they were on the way again, the two pairs of tracks thudding under the car's tyres before they picked up speed on the curving road. The boy watched as they passed a raupo-fringed lagoon where a pair of pūkeko picked their way with comic steps.

"We're just about in Tauranga," volunteered the man as they approached a low hill with a row of houses roosting along its top. "Where does your aunt live?"

The boy was ready for it.

"It's close to where the Auckland road goes out of the town," he said. "You can drop me off on your way out."

"What street?"

"Can't remember its name. But I know how to get there from the main road. It's close to the Auckland road," he repeated.

The car slowed to a halt at an intersection.

"Okay," said the man, "this is it. Now you're sure you know where to go from here?"

The boy took a quick look around.

"Sure," he answered, pointing to his left. "It's just up that road. Not far at all." He picked up the kit and pulled at the door handle.

"Thanks for the ride," he said before shutting the door, then giving a brief wave he turned and began to walk up the road he had indicated. The station wagon moved on, rolling down the slope to the city boundary. It was soon out of sight.

The boy retraced his steps and started descending the hill as the shadows began to lengthen in the afternoon sun. This time he was in luck. A car stopped beside him just as he passed the speed limit sign.

"Need a lift?" asked the lady on the passenger side.

"I'm going to Auckland," he replied.

The back door opened and he climbed in, settling the kit on the seat beside him.

"Got an aunty there," he said, "I'm going to stay with her."

Traveller was winner of The Keith Henderson Award for Short Story in 1979 broadcast on *Radio New Zealand* in August 1979 published in *Freelance*, anthology, 1979.

1900s later decades

Increased political commitment to abiding by the articles of the Treaty of Waitangi, the agreement made between the indigenous people and the British Crown in 1840, saw further addressing of past injustices to Māori in the later decades of the 1900s.

Immigration from a wider number of countries contributed more international flavour to society. In particular, a rise in the number of arrivals from other islands in the South Pacific – particularly Samoa, Tonga, Cook Islands, Niue, Fiji and Tokelau – boosted the country's identification as a Pacific nation.

Concern for human rights elsewhere resulted in New Zealanders voicing protest both at home and beyond their own shores. In the 1980s there was strong social action regarding French nuclear testing in the Pacific, and the policy of apartheid in South Africa.

OUR FAMILY, OUR ISLANDS

Mata pulled the basket of seafood toward her, steadied it between the rocks set into the earth for that purpose, and picked up the long-bladed knife reserved for opening shells. She beckoned to the children to come and join her, and waited while they picked their places on the tapa cloth set on the grass between her home and the beach – bigger ones sitting cross-legged at the back, little ones crawling at the front where some would fall asleep under her watchful eye. The older ones, she knew, would fidget, wanting to be off – into the plantation, running down to the shore and challenging each other to swimming races in the lagoon. But it was important they knew the tales of past times, and who else would tell them if she didn't.

"Settle down and pay attention now," she told them. The story she wanted to tell today was one they needed to know, even if they didn't understand it now. Perhaps it would come back to them in years to come, maybe after she'd gone, and at that time they'd grasp the meaning behind the words.

"This is the story of the three children of our family. It is how we tell it in our island of Te Motu Hōu."

When the firstborn arrived in the world she was first held up to the sky, then placed on the soil below, the skin of the Earth-Mother. Her colour was seen to be the same rich red-brown as her parent and she was given the name Kura to establish her link to the earth.

The birth cord of Kura was bitten off and the chants were spoken. A gift of a giant turtle was made to the deities. Then a great feast was held at which there was no sparing of the finest delicacies. Since this was way back, in the time of the sandalwood trees, the infant's limbs were rubbed with fragrant oil and, when her pito dropped off, the core of the stem of a young banana plant was rolled on her stomach and the chants were offered again.

The baby was laid on the finest mats that could be made – as fine as though the most tender inner bark of the a'u had been chosen, and it had been beaten by Hina-o-te-Marama herself. Then the tapa was set upon vines of maire, with flowers of the tiare placed about, so her bed was sweet-scented and suited to her high status. She was fed on rich breast milk. The best coconuts were chosen and scraped and the fine cream from them was mixed with the pick of the shrimps that were caught. Each day her features were pressed and moulded by expert fingers to ensure she acquired the admired attributes of beauty.

The child flourished, provided as she was with the best that the land had to offer. The sea beyond the reef that surrounded the island reflected changing shades from deep violet at dusk to the most iridescent blue when the sun stood highest. Day and night the waves washed onto the reef with a rhythmic roar. The lagoon provided seafood of endless variety and Kura was given the most succulent fish and crabs. From the lush green vegetation that grew on the ring of fertile land the sweetest bananas, and the pick of the yam and taro crops, were given to the growing maiden. Kura's ears were ornamented so that the lobes stretched, and she displayed the beauty and wisdom that was the ideal of the people at that time. Her clothing, crafted by the finest practitioners of the art, was of royal tapa.

It was in the time of the youthful maturity of Kura that the second of the three children of our family arrived. Unlike his sister, this one was not the colour of the rich earth when he was put upon it. A coconut was husked and cracked open and it was seen that his skin was as pale as the flesh within.

The navel cord of this child was cut and the pito placed in a gourd and sent out to sea. The child was then handed to the priests who washed him with water collected in a kape leaf and appropriate karakia were made. Makiri was the first name bestowed on this boy, though he was also known as Tane Ehu as he grew.

He was laid upon a bed of red cloth, his carers climbed the coconut trees for the best fruit and his limbs were massaged with hoho so he took on the scents of the land and its produce. It would be necessary said some, observing his colouring, to keep the lad indoors protected from the life of ordinary people in order to preserve and maintain the beauty of his pale skin. Others, though, argued that it was a gift of the gods and reflected his special status, and so could not be taken away. Makiri, therefore, was not shut away and remained with the people.

He too was given the best dishes – kūmara, yam, taro and banana. Though he grew well he did not attain the robust physical stature of most young men.

When the boy was approaching his maturity the priests, using a sprig of miro dipped in water collected in a giant clamshell, renewed his dedication to the great deity. Garlands of flowers were hung around his neck – the bright yellows, orange and red of the pua and the a'u.

From this time Makiri lost his liking for popoi and other cultivated foods and favoured different flavours – puaka, peka, tuna and tupa – so the people were sent out to satisfy his craving for the pig, bat, eel and crab. More and more Makiri preferred cooked food. He chose to massage his limbs with oil from the whale.

By this time in the story of our family, our people had ventured a distance across the ocean and left the first place, a low-lying atoll, behind. They were living on an island with rocky peaks in the centre and a circle of lowland and vegetation around it. In the old place Kura had always occupied the dwelling in the most prominent position but now, at Te Motu Tuarua, Makiri built a house in front of hers so now she could be seen to live in the house at the back. As time passed they-two grew further apart till it seemed they were no longer brother and sister.

Though in physical form Makiri was never the match of the other young men of the people he was set apart for the paleness of his skin. Since this was long regarded by the people as a sign of special status and beauty, his whims were not only tolerated but indulged. In his early manhood he took to wearing a scarlet girdle, and the strongest young men were sent out to climb the steep cliffs to the nesting grounds of the red-feathered vini to provide for his wants. The flocks of mamo too, were plundered, and Makiri's head was adorned with a headdress of a size and design not seen before.

Came the time, then, when he hungered for the fare of foreigners, particularly those who brought with them the mushroom. The brother, who more and more lusted after the new tastes, shunned the traditional foods – the ones that grew in abundance in the red-brown richness of the soil of Te Motu Tuarua.

By now they-two, Kura and Makiri, saw things each in their

own way. When dead fish were found floating in the lagoon Kura accused Makiri of poisoning the water with the grated nut of the utu. It seemed to her that the sound of the sea-waves on the reef was now a moaning, a call of anguish. That woman, in her distress at what had come to pass, considered preparing Makiri's canoe and sending him over the ocean to a distant place.

When the people began to fall down with diseases, and babies such as had never been seen before were delivered and died, Kura went again to the one who had been her brother. But Makiri, clad in girdle and headdress, stood with his back to her. With one hand under the other arm he thrust his elbow to his side and made the poko sound.

At this, the anger of Kura rose and she shouted at Makiri that all these bad things were the result of his desires and his changing of the order of things. The two stood up to each other, then locked in a fierce fight, each as they wrestled calling out the faults of the other, each accusing, taunting, attributing blame. Between the trees of the forest they fought and on the sand. In her rage Kura tore off a dead branch of a nono tree and plunged it into Makiri's left eye. Makiri scooped up a sharp piece of seashell and with it gouged Kura's eye. Both further incensed through their pain, they again locked in combat and tore out each other's remaining eye.

Now neither of the pair could see. They-two groaned and groped around in their blindness, scrabbling in the litter of forest and sand for further ways to maim each other. In their rage they tore out trees and tossed them about, they lifted rocks and threw them at where they believed the other was. When they came near each other they would lash out till eventually they both fell exhausted. A haze and then thicker cloud descended and settled on that part of the island.

After a time, they-two felt the pangs of real hunger gnawing at their insides and groped about in the darkness. Kura, finding the way to her plantation, fed herself on the plants she was able to pull and pluck. She heard the groaning of Makiri as his innards twisted and complained. At first she felt some satisfaction at his plight but as she listened she heard his continuing groans.

"He is still my brother," she thought, "and my brother is hungry." With that, she felt her way to him with a kete of food. When he had eaten Makiri crawled along the seashore and caught crabs that he placed in the basket for them both to eat. In this way the two survived their physical hunger.

But the chill mist still surrounded their world and its enveloping folds allowed the approach of other enemies. As they were sleeping on the beach Rori-nui-o-te-moana slid from the waters and up the sand to reach the pair. Kura felt the slimy skin of that monstrous sea slug as it sought to swallow her. At her scream Makiri felt for his maipi and wielding it wildly first cut off the tail of Rori. As Kura pulled herself free of the closing jaw another stroke of the weapon cut off its head.

The following day, in his blindness, Makiri did not see the fin of Mako-nui-o-te-moana cutting through the lagoon toward him as he searched for shellfish in the shallow water close to the shore. At the smell of the man, that monster had leapt the reef on an incoming wave. Kura, though, caught the smell of the great shark and called out to Makiri to run. Just in time her brother sprinted up the sand to avoid the grasping mouth with the rows of teeth.

They-two moved further up the beach and took care to have their weapons at hand. But Maroro-nui-o-te-moana-me-te-rangi propelled himself from the depth of the sea, flying over reef and lagoon, to they-two as they rested under the shade of the a'u. This time Kura heard the sound of fish-scales and fins as they passed through the air.

"Brother, take care, it is Maroro the flying fish." The maipi of Makiri swept through the sky above their heads and through the cooperation of the pair the monster fell dead at their feet.

They-two then, acting together to assist each other, made fire, prepared a cooking oven, and feasted on the bodies of those monsters that would have made Kura and Makiri food for themselves.

Mata paused in her narration to switch kete, replacing the spent basket with another. The account of the fight between the sister and brother had caught and held the interest of the older ones. Before they moved to leave the mat, she carried on.

"This story, though, is of the three children of our family, so listen, pay attention now to the part of the tale that concerns te pōtiki, the youngest – the one we call the Golden Child for the colour of its skin."

This one was born a little before the blindness of Kura and Makiri and it was during the time of the-mists-that-made-for-obscurity that this child was growing up.

In the infancy of the Golden Child, there was provided for its comfort a bed of soft down. The best of foods from far and wide were fetched, and the golden-skinned limbs were massaged with exotic sweet-scented oils. The perfumes in the ointments seduced the senses of the people so that they ignored the stench of what was lying beneath the mist in the hidden region of the land.

It was when the Golden Child reached maturity there rose the question, "Who are my kin?" Then the people remembered the older sister and the older brother and pointed to the forgotten area – the area that was not spoken of.

The Golden Child looked at the faces of her people and pondered on what had taken place within the family in the past. Coming to a conclusion, the Golden Child visited the sacred area and selected a single round stone, then fetched the finest pute and into this ornament basket placed tokens of the wealth of the people and the land – a headdress of splendid scarlet feathers, beautiful flowers and fruits, and portions of the choicest foods, together with the stone from the sacred place.

"My sister, my brother," called the Golden Child from just outside the hidden area, "I am te pōtiki, the youngest, your kin. Come out so that we might see each other."

Kura and Makiri recoiled as the sound reached them. It was a long time since they had heard any voice penetrating from beyond the mists of their enclosed world. They shook their heads, puzzling, striving to comprehend. The call came again. They tried to ignore it, but the message was repeated and insistent. Eventually they moved closer to the edge of the enveloping fog.

"My sister, my brother, come out so that we might see each other."

After a long time of calling by the Golden Child, Kura and Makiri emerged from the mist. The Golden Child pressed the nose of each making the hongi. They-two ran their hands, the brown of the earth and the white like the inside of the coconut, over the face of their sibling and felt its beauty. Only then did tears wash the blind eyes of Kura and Makiri.

The Golden Child, seeing the tears, reached into the bag and removed a nono fruit. The fruit was pressed to each of the blinded eyes in turn. Kura and Makiri blinked in the light and saw the youngest of their family, not as a baby as they remembered, but matured and standing tall and strong before them. They were amazed at the sheen of the golden skin of te pōtiki and marvelled at the brightness of the colours of the Golden Child's garment of pareu cloth.

Now they could again see, and as the mist slowly dispersed from the hidden area, they looked about and saw that the island they had known was not as before. Where they-two had fought during their blindness they could see great trees overturned – their roots in the air and their heads on the earth. Because of the rocks that had been thrown about, the landmarks they once knew were jumbled, the signs obscured. They could see that the way they had known had become confused. They hung their heads.

But the Golden Child led they-two back to the village and prepared a ceremonial fire so all could feast on the tapu-dispelling food.

Then, working together, they built a single large vaka. When it was constructed, they-all gathered on the shore and climbed on board. With the Golden Child standing at the prow, Kura, Makiri, and their people set out on a journey, arriving at an island of upraised coral. This island, Te Motu Hōu, had an encircling reef that gave the people protection from the might of the ocean and its monsters and provided a seafood basket within the lagoon. Most importantly, it was large enough to accommodate all. The children of our family built houses in a row around the shore and they lived side by side.

Mata picked up the last mollusc from the basket, flicked out the flesh into the plastic bowl, and threw the shell onto the heap already in the bucket. She looked over the group seated in front of her. Little Ailani, the youngest of the grandchildren was asleep, his honey-coloured body stretched across the lean legs of Lele, who was stroking his brow. She smiled and gave them a nod as she gathered the utensils to be carried to the kitchen. As the older ones scrambled to their feet she stopped them with a sign.

"This is the story of the children of our family to this time," she told them. "It is not concluded."

PROTESTOR

He caught her outside at the letterbox clearing the day's mail so, a little ungraciously, she agreed to hear him out. He followed her in the front door, vacuum cleaner grasped in one hand and a slim black case in the other.

Well, it was his lucky day, if not hers. Normally he wouldn't have a chance. She'd learned long ago to check the identity of callers if the doorbell rang when she was working. From behind the semi-sheer tone-on-tone curtains in the studio she could see the front door clearly, and she'd got know the sorts to ignore. Middle-aged or elderly couples, the man in a modest suit, woman with hat, and carrying a bag or briefcase – they were the worst. They'd be all ready, bookmark in Isaiah, and speeches better rehearsed than finalists at a beauty contest. Other salespeople were more obvious to pick by their cases of goods – and more stoppable, she'd found on the odd occasion one slipped through initial scrutiny.

That was the trouble with working from home. If she rented premises in the city most people wouldn't think of interrupting her during working hours, she complained to herself. But because her working space was in her own house, even her friends often refused to understand – after all, she was at home, wasn't she? She must have time. She wasn't the sort to be rude to callers, so precious time had often been wasted from the day. Hence the screening process from behind the curtains.

But this one had caught her outside, down the front path,

as she'd taken a brief break to pluck the day's post from the letterbox, and in a weak moment she agreed to let him in. No more than two minutes, he promised, and though she didn't believe it, she held the door open for him while he wiped his feet on the doormat. He moved into the lounge and put down the cleaner.

"What a pleasant room," he remarked, looking around. She knew it was the normal beginning to a sales pitch, but it pleased her anyway.

"Look, I'm quite satisfied with my present vacuum cleaner…" she began.

"Good," he replied, apparently unperturbed. "But I may as well test it for you while I'm here – there's no charge for that."

Now she was annoyed with herself for allowing him to waste her precious minutes, but she went out to get the cleaner, thinking as she did about the man's accent. She knew it well – her weeks in Johannesburg and Pretoria two years before had sensitized her to the giveaway vowels.

She returned with the cleaner and placed it on the lounge floor next to the new one. It looked a little shabby in comparison.

"Our old brown model, I see," said the man. The woman thought he emphasized the 'old' rather unnecessarily.

"I'm quite satisfied with it," she repeated. "It cleans well enough."

"Well let's try it, shall we," was the reply, the broad hands already unwinding the cord from around the handle. A confident glance around the room, and he picked out the wall-socket and plugged it in.

"I'll clean this area around your lounge suite with your cleaner," said the man, running the head across the area he indicated.

"Good carpet, this," he continued as he worked, "Have you got any idea what it would cost to replace?"

She didn't reply and began to feel very much on the defensive.

He finished the area, unplugged the machine, and pushed it to one side toward the piano. Then he plugged in his own machine and paused, looking at her.

"We cleaned this area," indicated by a sweep of his arm "with your cleaner. Did we not?" he asked.

The woman had the feeling she was being set up, as though by a magician. This lady has examined the rings. Now tell the audience if there are any breaks in them? She didn't reply. He didn't appear to notice.

"Now I'll go over the same area with the new machine, and we'll see what sort of a job your cleaner made of it." He touched his foot to the switch and ran the head over the carpet again. She watched – growing more and more irritable over the performance.

A minute later he finished, switched off the machine and asked if she could bring him a sheet of newspaper. She went into the kitchen and returned with a complete edition. The man placed it on the carpet, opened the cleaner and emptied the contents of the bag onto the paper. There was quite a pile.

"How do I know that wasn't in there before you began?" she asked. She knew the moment she said it that she'd been set up again. Like when you say to the magician – open up your other hand – only to find that too is empty.

"Yes, I thought you might ask that," said the man, obviously pleased with the outcome, "Well, I'll do it again."

He spent an excessive amount of time, she thought, shaking out the remainder of the dust particles onto the paper, then replaced the bag inside the cleaner and turned it on again. Once more he ran it over the same area around the settee, pushing the hose with one hand, standing upright – all the time looking at her, as though daring her to notice how effortless it was to operate this new, improved, super-efficient model.

"Look at the suction it's got," he said to her, demonstrating by attempting to lift the head from the surface. It clung, pulling the pile upward from the floor before it let go.

"Try it yourself," he invited, handing her the hose. She took it because she didn't know what else she could do, how to refuse. He was right – it did have far more suction than her older model.

He stopped the machine and removed the bag again, shaking it onto a clean sheet of newsprint. Once more the grey circle told its tale. He didn't need to say anything this time. A born salesman – knew just when to speak and when not. Rather, he began to show her the advantages of the redesigned cleaning head. All in one, this one – no need to carry different heads around the house and keep on changing them. Just a quick twist and there it is. Once again, she had to agree it was a great improvement.

Then he was running a practised eye around the room.

"Good carpet," he said again, "and there's a few years of wear left in it. If it's looked after, of course. Cost over a thousand dollars to redo this room, I reckon. At today's prices. It's going up every month too," he added. "Do you have the same right through the house?"

She nodded.

"Anywhere between five and ten thousand dollars then, right through. And that's just the cost now."

Without waiting for her to speak, he bent to his briefcase and unclipped it. Taking out a thick block of printed forms, he began to write.

"I've allowed you fifty dollars on the old cleaner – we won't make anything on it ourselves – that reduces the price of the new one..."

He ripped off the top copy and handed it to her.

"There you are – now that's not much of an outlay when you consider the investment you've got in the carpet, is it?"

She looked down at the figures written in blue ballpoint on the form. She felt trapped. He'd had it all his own way – set her up, laid all the traps, and she'd fallen into them. She was annoyed. Two minutes, he'd said, and it must have been nearer fifteen. Time was money as much to her as it was to him. She thought of the artwork waiting in the studio, and the deadline pressing.

"You have to admit it's a better cleaner than yours, don't you?" he asked.

She couldn't deny it. "Yes, it is," she admitted.

"And you would like to have one? Yes?" That accent again – it had been strong on the final word.

She took a breath. "Yes, I'd like to have one."

He beamed and reached into the case for another pad.

"But not that one," she added, "I'd like a – a red one."

He shook his head, smiling. "No, no – they're all the same colour. Your name please..."

She persisted. "But I don't like that colour," She kept her voice even, determined to sound calm, reasonable.

"Madam, I'm afraid you'll have to accept it all the same. We make one colour at a time, you see. Each new model has a different colour. Your old one is brown, the next model was blue, and now this is the newest one. But only one colour."

"Well then, I won't take it, thank you all the same," she said.

He was staring at her in amazement. "But Madam – does it really matter whether you like the colour or not?"

"Yes, it does," she replied, beginning to enjoy herself.

"But you said it worked better than your old one..."

"It does," she agreed, now willing to do so.

"The new model's a great improvement on the one you have now. You said it yourself."

"Yes, it's much better. The problem is the colour – I'm quite sure it's an excellent machine otherwise."

There was a moment's silence. Then, as though he'd just completed a count to ten, he spoke – slow and deliberate, each word placed.

"Do you mean to tell me, that knowing this machine will clean your carpet perfectly well, you won't take it – just because you don't like the colour?"

She smiled. "That's right."

He shook his head, unbelieving, and continued to move it to and fro as he picked up his belongings and walked to the door. The woman opened it for him, wished him good morning, and shut it again behind him.

She walked into the studio and settled herself on the high stool in front of her desk. Picking up a medium brush she continued her work where she had left off some time before. R-A-C-I-S-T-T-O-U-R she wrote, then held out the sheet to look at the result. Yes, that was quite satisfactory, she thought to herself. In fact, very satisfying all around. She'd done some good work this morning.

Protestor was broadcast on *Radio New Zealand*, first in December 1982.

WHAT A GUY, MAKES YOU CRY, AND I DID

It's after two o'clock in the morning and we're in the car outside the Hollywood in Avondale.

Most of the crowd from the picture show have gone but the two of us are still sitting here because it's taken Jenna some time to dig the keys out of her jeans pocket. Now she's trying to fit them into the ignition switch.

I push back a strand of damp hair that's fallen over my eyes. My skirt is still wet in streaks from the jets from the water pistols and there's a mess of black newsprint all over my hands from the copy of the *Star* I used to protect myself.

The last of the red tail lights are disappearing in the direction of the city. Jenna is still fumbling with the keys. She's singing.

Don't dream it – be it.

Don't dream it – be it.

Then I see this group of skinheads walking down the footpath toward us. Well, two of them are real skinheads, I see as they get closer. The one on the outside has a scalp full of dark bristles coming through. The tops of the others gleam pink and shiny in the light of the street lamp above.

I watch them as they go by. They don't look our way.

Then I'm getting out of the car without thinking and staring at their backs as they walk on. They're dressed in the same kind of gear – dark leather jackets and Doc Martin boots pulled over tight pants. One trails a long scarf that reaches down past his bum.

Eddy? I call out.

For a moment I don't think there's any response but then the middle one hesitates and the three stop. They just stand there with their backs to me. Not looking around.

Eddy. I call again. It's me – Rose. I use the name he knows me by.

I guess he says something to the ones on each side of him though I don't hear any words. The two walk on a few paces and stop by some motorbikes that are lined up at right angles to the curb so that their back wheels are just touching the raised concrete of the footpath. Eddy stays still while they move on then he turns, slowly, and takes a few steps toward me until we're about half a dozen paces apart.

And now I've called him back I just stand there not knowing what to do next.

I could say something like – Hey, I've often wondered if I'd ever run into you. Or, it is you isn't it? I thought I recognized you, but I wasn't certain.

Because it's been seven years. We never did talk much back then and somehow that habit carries over into now.

So, there it is. I'm standing just a few steps away from my brother and neither of us says a word.

It is Eddy – I'm sure of that now. In the way he's standing I can see him just as he used to look. But I'm not scared of him anymore. That feeling disappeared on the last day I saw him. The last day too that I saw my mother. It was the day she died.

She was the only person I ever remember saying something nice about Eddy.

Stand up for him next time someone says something about him, she used to tell me. He is your brother.

And I wish he wasn't, I shouted back more than once when I'd come home upset because my friends weren't allowed to come to my house the way I went to theirs.

It's all his fault, I'd cry. No one will come here because their mothers say he's always in trouble.

He's your brother, she'd repeat. Other people just don't know him the way we do. Families should stand up for each other. Eddy would do it for you if you needed him.

I never believed it then and, looking back, I wonder if she did either at the time. All she'd got back from him for years was shit. But she continued to defend him. On the occasions when Dad and he would almost come to blows she would stand between them. Leave him alone Ted, she'd say to my father – he's our son and he's a good boy.

Once, when things were really bad because of some trouble over a motorbike and Dad had threatened to kick him out of the house, I saw her cry. That was the time she told me about the teddy bear. About how when she came home from the hospital after having me she found Eddy had hacked a hole in his bear's body so that between its legs there was a big gap in its fur where the grey stuffing showed through. And how when she'd asked him why he did it he went into a rage and screamed over and over I hate teddy, I hate teddy.

Even after the trouble over the cannabis Mum continued to stand by him though she was the only one who did.

At school, when the other girls made remarks about the lot he went around with, I'd try to make out as though he wasn't anything to do with me and join in the talk about boys who hung around the streets on motorbikes and made it unsafe for girls to go out in the daytime let alone at night.

After Mum got sick Eddy spent less and less time at home till I often didn't see him for days on end. When she went into hospital for a long stay she used to ask for him, but I don't think he visited her very often. Perhaps he did during the day when I was at school. I didn't know or care. I had my own problems then.

That afternoon when he came home, and I told him she had died, he said I'm leaving I'm not staying here anymore. He went into his room and started throwing things around. I went after him and asked him not to go. I pleaded with him to stay because I didn't want to be there either anymore. Not alone with Dad. Eddy turned. He looked right into me and he saw.

You too, he said. I'll kill him. His hand went toward the leg where I knew his knife was strapped. He pushed past me to the door. For the first time in years I reached out to my brother. At that time I was more scared for him than of him.

Don't do anything, I begged. Please don't do anything. Things are bad enough now without making them worse. But he pushed past me and left the house. That was the last time I saw him. I didn't go to the trial.

So here we are. My brother and me. Standing just a few steps apart and still neither of us saying a word.

I hear the car start up beside me. Eddie looks toward it and then back at me.

How's it going for you? he asks.

All right, I answer. I'm okay.

Jenna has missed me. The driver's door opens and she leaps out. She runs around the front of the car and stands tall and dark by my side.

What's going on? she demands.

Eddy looks at her for a moment then nods his head before turning back toward his companions. He catches up to them where they've waited a short distance on, and the three of them walk away together.

I open the door and get in. Jenna slides into the other seat and sends out an unspoken question.

My brother, I reply.

She says nothing – just puts the gear-lever into first and wheels out into the empty street making a U-turn so we can head back to the city.

As we leave the theatre behind she is singing.

I'm going home

I'm going home.

MORNING IN SUBURBIA

Everyone in the group deferred to Pauline – "she's the one, you know, who ate her placenta."

Robina wasn't sure about the intricacies of placenta ownership, and the discussion around the room had suggested that it wasn't a strictly defined matter.

"With Sky, my placenta was so ragged the midwife couldn't be sure it was all there..."

"When I had my Zac, his placenta presented before he did."

Robina tried to imagine what a placenta looked like. The first image that came was like a piece of tripe and she shuddered, but then she remembered Snuffy's litter, and made it darker and smoother – more like a liver.

Her belly gave a lurch just as she leant sideways to her left to put her whispered question to her neighbour. Lorraine laughed and spoke aloud.

"Ask her yourself, she won't mind." When she noted Robina's hesitation she spoke again. "Pauline, Robina wants to know if you ate it raw, or whether you cooked it."

Knowing smiles around the circle showed that the story had been told before, probably retold over and over. On Robina's right, the woman who'd been introduced to her as Mere gave a snigger. "Here we go again", she said in a low but not inaudible voice.

Pauline paused to scoop up her toddler, unhook her blouse, and attach him to her breast, before she shared her experience.

She recited it as though she was imparting the secrets of an award-winning dish – lightly sautéed, very lightly, mind, so it's barely done through, in olive oil, best grade, of course, with just a sprinkling of tarragon over the top.

Robina, whose imagination had run to the indulgence of a rich gravy with cubes of bacon and a squeeze of orange juice, felt let down by its simplicity. Her following thoughts of oranges, her past craving for them, and the memory of the woman with the hennaed hair at Natural Foods for Natural Health were interrupted by a question from a young woman across the room. Her face had displayed horrified fascination as Pauline spoke, and now she blurted out –

"But wouldn't that be, like, cannibalism?"

Pauline had obviously met this one before. Her smile was tolerant, a little superior.

"Of course not," she said, "it's not as though the placenta has a life of its own. It helps to nourish life – it's full of nutrients supplied by the mother. What's more natural than the mother taking this back into herself."

Robina thought of the henna-haired woman and her advice that the body tells you what it needs, you only need listen, and if Robina had a craving for oranges then her body was telling her she needed more vitamin C, or perhaps potassium, and it was lucky for her that she'd come in when she did because right now this supplement which the hennaed woman recommended had an extra ten per cent more tablets for the same price, for a limited period only.

Pauline was continuing with the observation that the practice was common in animals. A mother cat, for instance, would eat a kitten's placenta, which obviously showed that it contained nutrients she needed following the birth. The low-toned voice to Robina's right commented that it might also suggest an instinctive protection and survival tactic – the quick removal of the afterbirth being designed to avoid attracting predators.

"Perhaps," purred Pauline, not deterred, clearly favouring her own interpretation.

The hostess moved around the group offering a variety of teas on a tray.

"How far on are you, dear?" she asked Robina. "Then here, take this one – it's a special herbal blend I mix myself. I found it marvellous in my last trimester."

Forty minutes later, as Robina turned left at the gate and started to walk the block and a half to her own home, a voice spoke behind her.

"You're not thinking of doing it, are you?" Mere again. "You know, eat the placenta," she added as Robina looked at her.

"I shouldn't think so. I don't expect to even see it. I've decided to go to hospital."

"Good for you," said Mere, "though not many of the ones there this morning would agree with you."

"Would you? Eat it. I mean?"

"God no," said Mere, "Anyway, I'm a vegetarian. Well, most of the time – except when I'm at the marae – it's hard to be a veggie there."

They walked for a minute in silence.

"My family still buries it." Seeing Robina's puzzled look, Mere added "The placenta, and the umbilical cord. It's an ancient tradition to bury it. I know where mine is – under the kouka, the cabbage tree, by the old house. My husband thinks that's a great joke – tells people I was found under a cabbage plant."

Robina grinned. Mere let out a peal of laughter.

"Except it's not there. The real joke is that it's not there at all. My mother always thought it was, but my uncle told me the truth – one night when he'd had a few. When I was born, my mother asked the doctor for the whenua and gave it to my Nanny to take home and bury. She dug it in under the kouka. The next morning, though, my uncle saw the puppy was playing with something. He didn't take much notice – till a bit later when he found the hole, and the scratched out dirt. By then it was too late."

"The dog ate it?" asked Robina. "What happened?"

"Well, my Dad and my uncle, they considered killing the puppy and burying it under the tree, but then they'd have to tell Mum and Nanny what had happened. So they kept quiet. Neither of them ever knew."

Robina considered the facts in silence. She didn't know what to say. Until a fortnight ago, at the last antenatal class, the word placenta had no real relevance in her life. In a multi-choice knowledge test she may even have ticked the box by "open area in the middle of a shopping complex". Now it appeared to be yet another thing demanding she make a decision.

Mere had been silent too.

"You know that puppy," she said in a quieter voice, "as I grew up, she was devoted to me – watched out for me. When I was three I wandered off on my own at my grandparents' place and fell into a pond. Tiaki wasn't too keen on water, but she leapt in and pulled me onto the bank."

Robina stopped at her driveway. "Are you going to the group again next Thursday?" she asked.

"I'll see. I go only sometimes. It's a bit more than I can take every week," said Mere with an expression between a grin and a grimace.

"Is that true about your dog?"

Mere gave a throaty laugh. "That's what I was told. It makes a better story than Pauline's, eh? Kia kaha," she said, and continued on her way.

Morning in Suburbia was published in *Takahe* magazine, Spring 1995; a theatre version was staged in the Auckland Short and Sweet festival 2011.

IT'S ME, RAKU

Sitting there, with the grey strap stretched tight across his puku, Raku wanted to stand up and shout,

"Hey look – it's me, Raku, and I'm on my way."

But a middle-aged couple was settling in to the seats beside him – their necks garlanded with pink and white blooms. The air was heavy with the scent of frangipani. Then a stewardess was beside them in the aisle, handing out fruit juice in small clear cups. He took his and drank it. It left a cold feeling in his stomach, and his bare arms prickled under the stream of cool air blowing onto him.

The sound of loud laughter behind caused him to twist around and look through the small gap between the seat backs, but he could get only a glimpse of unfamiliar pale faces. He pulled at the clasp of the belt in his lap and half stood. The others were three rows back – he could see them there, his cousins, fooling and laughing together. He gave them a quick wave, then sat down again with a start as the plane began to move.

Another stewardess was standing in the aisle, wearing a life jacket and miming in time to a recorded message. Her dress was in shades of blue, with wavy lines – like the sea out beyond the coral reef.

The plane poised, quivering, at the end of the runway, then they were racing along the tarmac and lifting into the air, over the tops of the coconut trees, the houses, and past the hospital on the hillside at the point. And again he wanted to shout,

"It's me, Raku, and I'm on my way."

The lady beside him was leaning over, trying to catch a view of the island as the plane banked. He caught her eye as he glanced back, and she gave a self-conscious smile.

"Is this your first time off the island – away from home?" she asked a few moments later.

He nodded. "Yes," then volunteered, "I'm going to live in Auckland."

"What part?"

"New Lynn."

"You've got relatives to go to?" It was more a statement than a question.

He nodded again. The woman's husband leaned forward to look at him.

"You'll find it cold," he warned, "I hope you've got something warmer to put on."

Raku indicated the shell bag at his feet, which held the garment given to him by an uncle who had come back some months ago. "I've got a jersey in there," he assured them.

The man laughed. "It'll need to be a thick one at this time of year," he said, and picked up his book. The lady pulled the flight magazine from the seat pocket in front of her and began to read.

After a while Raku did the same. His copy was still sealed in a plastic bag, along with postcards and a green plastic tiki. He left the small items in the bag and placed it in his kit. When he got to Auckland he'd send one of the postcards back home – in an envelope with the tiki. The kids would like that.

He flipped over the pages of the magazine, looking at the full colour photos. He absorbed the images, then let his mind wander ahead – to Auckland as he imagined it. The shops, the streets full of cars, huge halls and picture theatres full of people. A job, and plenty of money in his pocket.

His cousins had told him all about it when they came back home for a while. Not just with words. But by the way they talked and acted – the way they dressed in their good clothes. And most of all, the way they couldn't settle again to the island life and looked forward to going back. Sometimes, when they'd been enjoying themselves – swimming in the lagoon, or filling their stomachs at a family feast – they'd look at each other and say, "It's better here – let's not go back to New Zealand." But then they'd laugh, as though it was a private joke, and they were all a part of it.

After the meal was served, he brought out the magazine again and read the articles right through, paying particular attention to the pictures of his new country. His new country. It gave him a good feeling to think like that, and in his thoughts he could hear the family at home talking. "Raku – he lives in New Zealand now."

Then the plane was circling over the city. Looking down, Raku was at once scared and excited at the size of it all. His stomach was full of European food, and now he was a part of it too. As they thumped down onto the grey surface he whispered to himself,

"It's me, Raku – and I'm there."

* * * * * * *

He was by himself this time, with no cousins three rows back. It was just Raku – but different.

This time there was no nervous excitement as the plane taxied and then lifted into the air, turning to the north, away from the city. When he spoke to the stewardess and the other passengers beside him, it was in a more assured manner than he could have once imagined. And when he reached home they would exclaim over how he looked – how tall he had grown in the past few years, and how smart he was in his New Zealand clothes.

He was lucky to have the window seat again. Not that there was anything to see so many thousands of metres above the Pacific, but he could prop his head on a pillow against the wall of the cabin and shut his eyes. And he could think. Think about what he would say when he was back home. How he would answer the questions – especially that one he knew they would ask first.

"Are you home for good, or are you going back?"

What would he say when they asked him about New Zealand? He could tell them about the streets full of houses – block after block, mile after mile. And the football matches at the parks where there was seating for more than ten, twenty, fifty times the number of people on their whole island.

Or he could talk about his job – the steady job that gave him plenty of money in his pocket every week. Would he tell them that for most of these years he stood and watched a machine that punched out tin cans – hour after hour, day after day? And that he'd been called Ron, because the foreman wouldn't make the effort to pronounce his name? That at the factory Sione was Sam, and Tamarua was Ted?

Raku opened his eyes as he heard himself being spoken to. A blue-suited steward was holding out a tray of food to him. He stretched out his hand, then let it drop. "No thanks," he said, "I'm not hungry." His head found the pillow again, and his eyes closed.

His mind went back to the time last year when he was sick for that week. All he had been able to do for those days was lie with his head on a sweat-drenched pillow, eating nothing, his head a pounding pain that could find no relief. The medicine that the doctor left had no effect, and he remembered how he wanted to die when the fever was at its worst. Even when the virus had passed, he had been weak for several more days, and when he could eventually go back to work it was a surly reception that greeted him, with the foreman asking if he was sure it suited him to work this week.

"All the same, you coconuts," was the muttered remark as the man moved off.

Would he tell them about that at home? And about the man he worked with, who kept asking if he had saved enough money yet to build a concrete house back in his village? They were a good bunch though, who had once passed the hat around for one of their gang who had got into a scrap at the hotel and couldn't pay a fine. Raku had often wondered how these men lived – what their homes were like inside, and how they talked to their families.

Then he wondered if those at home would believe him anyway if he told them about some of these things. He thought back to how he used to be, listening to his cousins. Did they tell him about these things, and did he listen? He remembered only the vivid descriptions of the places, the people, the parties, and how he wanted so much to be a part of it.

It would be the same for the others now. Especially when he handed out the gifts from his bulging suitcases. He could tell them about the foreman, but they wouldn't be interested. The older ones would just want to hear about the amount of money he had in his pocket every week – about the way the shops were always full, with no shortages of sugar or cans of corned beef because the boat hadn't arrived. The kids, they would want to hear over and over about the picture theatres, the carnivals, and the glitter of K Road on late shopping night.

He shrugged his shoulders. He'd tell them about all those things – and about the ice cream parlours, the pizza shops, and the takeaway bars that are open till all hours of the night. About how they'd start off a Saturday evening with a session at a movie theatre, follow it up at a disco, and then all get hamburger and chips to eat on their way home. And the kids would sit there amazed that he'd come back, because they'd be sure it was paradise – the way he had once done.

For a while he slept. When he woke he was aware that the plane was descending, and soon they were slipping through white wisps of cloud as they dropped. People around him were putting away books and writing paper, and checking passports and landing cards. Raku sat up and removed his jacket, folding it before he stowed it in the airline bag on which he had rested his brown polished shoes. How they would admire that jacket at home, and whistle when he told them how much it cost. Not so much at the amount, but at the fact that he, Raku, could afford it.

The people in the row ahead were pointing out of the window. In the distance and far below he could see the island – its mountains rising from the shades of blue that stretched as far as he could see. He tried to imagine what his family would be doing down there. Perhaps they'd look up at the plane and wonder if it brought a letter from him. He hadn't told them he was coming – it would be a surprise when he walked in. Again, he wondered what he would answer to the question they would ask first.

Quite close now, off to his right, he could see the blue of the lagoon and the white waves breaking over the reef, the hospital, then the iron roofs of the houses, most of them rusty and dilapidated. Here was the airport now, with its fringe of lush green kept in check by the distant wire fence. He anticipated the bump, and it came right on cue.

A wave of feeling passed over him, and he found he wanted to stand up and shout,

"It's me, Raku – and I'm home!"

It's Me, Raku was published in *The Bay of Plenty Times,* 28 May 1983.

SHELLS

*In the beginning, according to tradition on our island,
there was void.
To the void itself there was no beginning.
It simply was.*

When I was a young girl I lay on the beach at night and looked up into the dark sky. Far above there were a million stars – as many as the shells that glisten on the wet sand as the tide abandons them to return to the calling sea. All around was the constant rustle of the palms as the breezes brushed through their branches. And of course, there was always the sound of the waves breaking on the reef.

Uncle Ratu said void was nothing at all. I tried to imagine what that was like. When we went out to sea, way beyond the reef, even if we went right out of sight of land, there was still sky and water. And the canoe. This was closer, because Uncle Ratu said on some Pacific islands they say that in the beginning there was nothing except water. Everywhere water. No horizon over which an island, no matter how small, could be lying. No separation. Only water.

"You mean, void is when there is no land? Just water?"

"Void is no water either. Nothing."

"Just sky, then?"

"Sky is something. Void is the absence of everything. Nothing at all."

I closed my eyes and stripped out all the sights I knew. Even with my eyes shut tight I was aware of something. The laughter of the younger children playing, a thud of a coconut as it hit the ground. There was nowhere I could go to escape the sea breeze and the sound of the water washing onto the sand.

The more I thought about it the less I could understand nothing. Aunty Taina laughed.

"Hina, there you go again, girl, trying to understand everything before you've experienced anything. Give yourself time." She scooped me into her large arms, but I broke free and went and sat on the branch that overhung the lagoon to think.

> *Then an egg existed in the primal void.*
> *To the egg itself there was no beginning, it simply was.*
> *It existed for aeons.*
> *There was a time of settling.*
> *Within the settling Matua, the Source of All Things,*
> *existed in the egg.*
> *Existed for aeons.*
> *The egg grew, cracked, and the parent of all emerged.*
> *Matua, glorious in scarlet feathers, took half the shell*
> *and lifted it up on high*
> *to form the dome of Sky above the mound of Earth.*
> *Then using the attributes of its own being, the Source of*
> *All Things,*
> *called forth the elements of existence.*

Perched on my branch, I pondered the logic, but Uncle Ratu and the others insisted that it was the atua who gave us these stories so there was truth in them.

It is said that after being alone for countless ages,
the Parent yearned for company.
Into the primal sea Matua threw an egg-shaped
boulder,
then another, and another.
They became land. Our islands.

"It is time Hina went to her father's people," said Aunty Taina to the aunties one day. "There she will go to a proper school. Hina is clever and deserves to be educated." The aunties nodded, and the uncles agreed it should be so.

The next time the big boat came I was put on board, with one of the aunties to keep me company on the three-day trip. Away from the atoll there was water as far as I could see, but still there was sky and sea, and the line of separation between them.

After a long time, Matua looked down at the islands
that had formed.
They were bare. So Matua threw down a twig, which
grew into a vine.
The vine flourished and eventually covered the land.
When parts broke off and decayed, maggots formed in
the rotting wood.
Matua took the maggots and gave to each of them first
a heart,
then limbs, and then a soul.
The maggots became the first people.

The year I sat the entrance examination for high school was the year of the big debate that arose after an argument between a journalist and the head of one of the churches. The subject gripped the island. Newspaper columns and letters-to-the-editor were full of it, churches and school halls were packed for night time meetings. Feelings ran high as people argued whether creation occurred in one big bang, six days, or billions of years. Families and friends argued, and rumours were rife that the burning of two houses belonging to lay-preachers in one village was the work of opponents in another.

On Uncle Pita's instruction we in the family avoided giving any opinion. Depending on the content of his editorials, we were either commended or condemned on an almost daily basis – often by the same people in quick succession. With a family as diverse as ours, said Uncle Pita, the only way to keep the peace was to stay out of the argument.

The peak of the controversy coincided with the time of the primary schools' annual oratory contest. I had been selected as representative of our school, and with one week to go the contestants were given the set topic – "The Creation". My heart sank.

"Eeii," said Aunty Maata, "what are you going to say? Better for you if you don't do it, girl. You know that Father Gerard is the chief judge."

"Hina wants to get into the College of St Mary the Virgin next year," said Aunt Tuli. "It's the best school on any of the islands."

"Eeeiii." Aunty Maata put down the dye for the tapa she and Tuli were working on. "What does Paoro think about that? How can the niece of the minister go to Saint Mary's?"

Aunt Tuli put her arms around me and quoted the proverb of the coconut and the crab.

"Do what you think is best for you," she told me, "this family is strong. It might rock a little, but it will stand."

*When Matua lifted the dome of Sky above the shell of
Earth,
between the two halves, in the division, it was dark,
for the hemispheres were held together by a great
octopus.*

On the day of the contest I sat on the dais listening to the
other speakers and watching the reaction of the adjudicators.
In three cases Father Gerard sat looking stern, arms folded over
the crucifix that hung on his chest. For the fourth, the entrant
from St Thérèse's, he clicked his pen more and more as the
boy stumbled over words which had obviously been carefully
dictated but barely rehearsed. I was the final speaker, and no
doubt something of a puzzle to audience and judges alike. As
I stepped to the front of the platform I could see the aunties
sitting three rows back were fanning themselves. Taking a deep
breath, I began –

"In the beginning there was void. Then an egg existed in the
primal nothingness. The egg grew, and it cracked, and Matua
emerged."

At the end of my final year at the College of St Mary the
Virgin, Father Gerard called me into his office and handed me
a letter. He pointed a finger at the familiar logo at the top.

"You start work in the laboratory next Monday. You are lucky
to get this chance. I've told the director you're the best pupil the
school has – don't let us down."

That was it. My career decided for me. There was no time to
go back to the island of my birth to see Aunty Taina and Uncle
Ratu after all. The following week I started work as instructed.

"Hina, come and look at this," Pierre called to me one day

across the laboratory. I left my work of testing soil and seawater samples to go to his bench, and looked into the microscope as he indicated.

"Creation in process," he breathed as I observed the activity through the eyepiece. "The first time I saw cells dividing I felt I was witnessing an act of God. It is strange, is it not, that in order for creation to take place there must first be disintegration – a separation in the original unit?"

> *The deities, the children of Matua-Atea and*
> *Matua-Papa,*
> *in rebellion at the restricted lives they were forced to live*
> *in the dark cramped conditions between the bodies of*
> *their parents,*
> *cut away the body of Atea from the tentacles of the*
> *octopus.*
> *They thrust the pair apart*
> *so that light could penetrate into the space between*
> *them.*
> *It is said that the two, Matua-Atea and Matua-Papa,*
> *still mourn that they must spend their time apart,*
> *viewing each other from such a distance.*
> *Since then, storms of wind and rain continue to lash the*
> *space between,*
> *forcing people to take shelter on the body of the mother.*

It was at the laboratory that I met Tane, one of the men who worked at the base on the atoll way out in the ocean in the opposite direction to my island of birth. They would all come into the lab every month for their tests.

The first time we sat on the beach together and looked up

at the night sky there were lights and noise all around. People walked above us on the esplanade; from a bar on one side came dance music, and the sound of jazz spilled out from the tourist hotel on the other. Tane appeared to be oblivious to it all. Even in a crowd he seemed to create his own space.

"In the beginning," he said, "there was chaos…"

"Chaos," I asked, "not void?"

"Chaos," he repeated. "Energy, form, matter – but not separated. Then there occurred settling and division. After that came attraction, or love, and from that there developed order." He took my hand in his.

"Hina," said Aunt Tuli, "sit down. I have a story to tell you." She and Aunt Maata were shelling hard-boiled eggs in preparation for lunch next day. It was always this way on a Saturday – as much as possible done ahead so that little remained to be done on Sunday.

"It was a long time ago," said Aunt Tuli.

"A long time," agreed Aunt Maata, "way back before your great grandfather's time, because I remember him telling us how it had happened in the generations before."

"There was a man, an ancestor of ours, who was to marry a woman from another group of islands. It had been arranged for a long time, since the two were small children. It was to be an importance alliance between our people and theirs. The day was planned, and all was ready for the arrival of the woman and her party. The day came, and the day went, for the party never arrived. Several days passed, then a delegation arrived. Without the bride."

"Eeeiii – without the bride. She had run away some days before with her lover."

"It was a bad thing – mana was lost, lives had to be taken. There has been bad feeling between these peoples ever since."

There was a pause in the telling. The aunts ceased their shelling and looked at me. The meaning was clear from their faces.

"Our people and Tane's," I said. The aunts gave each other a look and went on with their task.

"In the tradition of my mother's people," said Tane as his arms clasped me, "Father Sky and Mother Earth were held in a tight embrace by an octopus."

Uncle Ratu and Aunt Taina came on the big boat, and then others began to arrive. Each month as the ship tied up more of my mother's people came ashore, carrying their mats and other possessions all tied together.

"It's just till the sea goes down again," they said, "and the gardens lose the salt and are fertile again. Then we will go back."

With the help of Tane, my cousin Matiu was given a job with the company. Tane never talked about what they did at the base on the atoll, but now Matiu would come back full of praise for how he handled his squad of men. Tane, he said, was always at the forefront of the work – the first in and the last out. The aunties' looks softened as they worked together on Saturdays and Tane came to pick me up. Aunt Taina laughed.

"What did you expect from that one?" she asked Tuli and Maata, cracking an egg on the side of the enamel bowl. "The crab and the coconut, nei?"

When light penetrated between the bodies of Matua-
Papa and Matua-Atea
the gods saw that all that was revealed was not perfect.

Some things were ugly and misshapen.
So in the heavens they placed stars to shine.
On the land they put plants in a multitude of sizes and
colours,
and animals of different shapes and uses were formed.
Then the gods gave colours to the fish of the sea.

This past Sunday, in the morning, I was waiting outside the church. Waiting for Tane. The organ was playing and everyone else had gone in. Aunt Tuli came out looking for me.

"Aren't you coming in?" she asked.

"Not yet Aunty."

"Your uncle is about to start the service."

"You go back in," I said.

"Are you waiting for Tane?"

"I'll come in when he gets here."

"Perhaps he's not coming today."

"He will." I was sure of it. "The transport from the base must be late."

"You didn't eat this morning, Hina." Aunt Tuli put her arm around my shoulders

"I didn't feel like it."

"Or yesterday." Tuli put her other hand, the one holding her hymn book, on my stomach. I buried my head in her shoulder.

"What will Uncle say?"

Tuli hugged me close to her.

"You leave Paoro to me. We will work it out."

I heard Uncle begin the service, then the voices of the congregation as the first hymn began, but still Tane had not arrived. I had my foot on the step of the porch, my hand clasped in Tuli's, when Matiu came up behind me.

"Hina," he said too quickly as I turned, "it's Tane. They put him on the plane out last night. His tests were positive, and he's been sent to France for treatment. He'll be half-way to Europe by now."

My foot slipped off the step and I sank to my knees onto the grass beside the path. As I sat down I felt a warm rush between my legs and looked to see a red stain spreading on the skirt of my white dress.

Numberless are the shells of the world
since Matua emerged from the primal egg –
the shell of space and that of land,
those of the creatures of sky and earth.
Man's first shell is woman.
Woman's shell is also woman.

"A woman's shell," said Aunt Taina as she tended me, "is the most easily broken."

The Source of All Things
– the one who in these scattered islands has many
names –
populated and clad the Earth by self-sacrifice.
Spine and ribs became the mountains and reefs.
From the nails of fingers and toes came fish and
shellfish for the oceans.
Eels, lobsters and crabs were formed from the intestines.
The bright scarlet feathers are still seen in the plants.
The very earth was enriched and made productive by
the divine flesh.

Best of all, I used to think as a child sitting on my branch watching the sun set over the lagoon, the blood of the Source of All Things went to colour the morning and evening sky and the rainbow.

Now I lie on the sand among the mass of broken shells staring out at the expanse of sea that stretches into the sky so there seems to be infinite distance. I think of beginnings and endings, of order, love, and chaos.

"First there was Tane," I say to myself, "then there was an egg, and now there is void."

Shells was published in *Takahe 49*, Autumn 2003.

THE ASSUMPTION OF MARY

The first time the Blessed Virgin appeared to Clare she seemed to be in a pastoral setting, even though the place of the vision was C3 the maths room, and she was actually just to the right of the blackboard, hovering about halfway up. Sister Thomas, who was explaining simultaneous equations by means of strings of chalked symbols, did not seem to notice the divine vision less than a metre away. From a lack of appropriate reaction around her, which she imagined should at least have involved most of her class-mates abandoning their calculations and falling to their knees in a chorus of 'Hail Marys', Clare assumed that no one else in the room did either.

On the way home Thérèse was sceptical.

"Why would the Blessed Virgin appear to you? She'd be much more likely to come to me."

"You didn't see her then?"

"No, and I don't believe you did either. You couldn't – you're not even a Catholic." That seemed to be that. If the idea disturbed her friend, Clare decided it was best to leave the matter there. The pair walked on in silence.

"What did she look like?" Thérèse asked next day on the way to school.

"Who, Mary?" asked Clare.

"The Blessed Virgin Mary – that's what you should call her. You'd know that if you were a Catholic."

"She looked just like the picture on your bedroom wall."

"In a blue gown? With a gold crown on her head?"

"Yes, and with her hand on her heart, like this."

"I still don't believe you saw her. You can't." Thérèse's pronouncement was definite.

Each of the following appearances was similar. The Blessed Virgin simply sat looking at her for some minutes, benevolently Clare thought, before fading slowly from sight.

"Doesn't she say anything?" asked Thérèse.

"No, she just smiles."

"You see," pronounced Thérèse "if you were Catholic she'd give you a message – like she did at Fatima, or at Lourdes to Saint Bernadette. You could meet the Pope, to tell him what she said. But I still don't believe you."

"She wouldn't, would she, Mum?" Thérèse demanded confirmation of her judgement as the two girls sat at the kitchen table after school.

June Cecilly Martin, named a little short of four decades previously for her two grandmothers, but only ever referred to, or answering to, Julie, in order not to give any measure of preference to either, considered the several significances of the question.

"Why wouldn't she?" she asked.

"Because Clare's not a Catholic. The Blessed Virgin would come to me, not to her." In evidence and support of her claim Thérèse followed with a flawlessly delivered, if somewhat rapidly rendered:

Hail, Mary, full of grace, the Lord is with thee; blessed art thou among women, and blessed is the fruit of thy womb, Jesus.

Holy Mary, mother of God, pray for us sinners now and at the hour of our death. Amen.

She dipped onto one knee and crossed herself.

"There," she concluded, reseating herself on the rimu-look chair made environmentally-acceptable by the fact that it was actually pine treated to a rimu finish.

"Well, now," said June Cecilly, aka (*always* known as) Julie, "we wouldn't want to suppose, would we, that the Blessed Virgin is true only for Catholics?"

The next time she-who-is-blessed-among-women showed herself, she smiled and then lifted her hand from her breast and held it out in a gesture of blessing.

"I know," said Thérèse two days later between classes, "the Blessed Virgin *thinks* you are Catholic. I mean, she would, wouldn't she?"

"Why would she?"

"Because you're at St Mary's."

"Lots of people here aren't Catholics."

"Then there are your Christian names. Clare Elizabeth Mary. All saints' names." Thérèse, whose other given names were Mary Stacey, was acutely aware of the presence of an unsanctified interloper among her own list.

"I don't think my parents knew that," said Clare.

"That makes no difference." Thérèse had it all worked out. "And when is your birthday?"

"August the fifteenth. You know that."

"There you are – the Assumption of Mary. The Blessed Virgin's own Feast Day. Besides," she added, "she would think so because you're my friend. We're always together, and she knows I belong to the Church." Thérèse, triumphant in her epiphany, linked her arm through Clare's and kept it there till they were in the door of C3 and at their desks.

"Why did you call me Clare Elizabeth Mary?" Clare put the question to her mother as the two prepared the salad that evening.

Emma Nicola Sanderson, who had never experienced any notions of disappointment, disapproval, or even discontent over her given names, and therefore, on the occasion of the naming of her own daughter, had no strong views on what was or was not advisable, had taken a line of minimal resistance when faced with family pressure.

"Clare because I liked the sound of it, Elizabeth for your father's sister who died as a baby, and Mary because Nana Cochrane would have been very hurt not to get a look in there somewhere. You were her first great-grandchild. I've told you all this before," said Clare's mother, "why are you asking now?"

"Thérèse says they are all names of saints."

"Well, that could be, but I didn't know it at the time, so it's just a coincidence."

"Are you sure we're not Catholic?"

"Quite sure. Why?"

"And Dad's family? They're not Catholics?"

"I'm even surer about that. You know your Uncle Robert and what he always says."

"So I go to St Mary's just because it's closest?"

"That, and because Sister Elizabeth is the best music teacher in the region."

"Mum?"

"What now?"

"Do you think the Blessed Virgin Mary could make a mistake?"

"What sort of mistake?"

"Not know something – get something wrong?"

"I've no idea. You'll have to ask one of the Sisters. Now set the table for me."

Sister Julian, having secretly harboured a desire to have her own baptismal name, Christine, considered not only acceptable but even appropriate for one entering into a lifelong commitment as a Bride of Christ, had spent the first half of her years in the order trying to overcome the sin of resentment and accept the name given to her on ordination. The eventual resolution had been assisted by meditation on the collected works of Dame Julian of Norwich, judged suitable for study since the sweeping changes following Vatican Two.

"Well, Clare, that's an interesting question from one of our girls who is not of the Catholic family." Sister Julian smiled at Clare to show she meant no offence. "Would this be prompted by some argument on a particular point of doctrine?"

"No, Sister, I was just wondering. Could Mary, I mean the Blessed Virgin, mistake me for another person. For instance," she added.

"So, just a little human error – is that what you are asking?"

"I suppose so, Sister."

"Let me see." Sister Julian steepled her fingers and took a moment in thought before she responded. "You know that in the view of the Church the Blessed Virgin is the Holy Queen, Mother of Mercy, our Gracious Advocate who answers all who call on her?"

"Yes, I think so."

"Then I don't suppose she would be likely to make simple mistakes, do you?"

Thérèse, who had since thought through the implications, and was now adamant in her rejection of anything that might suggest less than one hundred per cent infallibility in the Mother of God, despite the fact that she was herself the initiator of the notion, agreed.

"So, Sister said the Blessed Virgin wouldn't make a simple mistake?"

"Yes."

"There you are – nuns don't tell lies."

The fifth appearance occurred during Friday afternoon art period when, under the tutelage of an ageing Sister Carmel who had long since ceased to remember that she had ever been called anything else, the girls were dispersed around the perimeter of the playing field with orders to capture the likeness of various trees. This time the B.V.M. was seated about a third of the way up the ginkgo. Clare's pencil paused over her art-block as she wondered for a moment whether she should include the figure in her sketch even though the instruction had been to depict only the tree itself, giving particular attention to its shape.

Clare opened her mouth, then shut it again as she stopped to wonder if it was proper to speak to a divine person and, if so, what was the correct form of address. Thérèse called her The Blessed Virgin, Mother of God, and Holy Queen of Heaven. The Pope was His Holiness, the Queen was Her Majesty, but Clare was sure the very Mother of God would outstrip any worldly rank. She scrambled from her cross-legged sitting position and knelt on the grass.

"Your Holy Majesty, Blessed Virgin, Mother of God, Holy Queen of Heaven," they all tumbled out as Clare attempted to cover the bases, "I'm Clare Elizabeth Mary Sanderson."

The blue-clad figure raised her right hand from her breast and extended it toward the kneeling girl.

"Excuse me, but I'd like to know, if you know that I'm not a Catholic?"

The Virgin's hands clapped together in front of her heart, her eyes widened, and her mouth opened a little. Then she was gone.

On Monday afternoon when most of the other students had left the school grounds, Clare raised her hand and knocked on the door which, true to its appearance, was oak varnished to a golden gloss. A trinity of lies weighed on her conscience.

The first, was telling Sister Carmel that a bad headache was the reason for her abandoning Friday's art class with no result on the sketch block. The second was repeating the same story to Thérèse three hours later to avoid their trip to Cinema 8. Tom Cruise, she had surprised herself by thinking, would still be there next weekend. At the time she was not so sure about Thérèse should she confess the truth – that she had offended the very Mother of God. Clare was not sure whether telling a lie to a nun was worse than fibbing to her closest friend, though she felt sure Thérèse would think so. It was Thérèse's feelings, however, which concerned her more. So lie number three, the one that had occupied her thoughts all weekend, the big one in theological terms, remained untold, to become a sin of thought rather than commission. Recanting her past claims, saying the visions had been a figment of her imagination, had at first appeared the easiest way out. The only way out, it seemed, and Clare was prepared to do that to preserve the two girls' friendship. Until Sunday night when a further thought led to Clare kneeling by her bedside.

"Your Holy Majesty, Blessed Virgin, Mother of God, Holy Queen of Heaven," she started again, as preamble to her rehearsed statement.

As Clare opened the tall oak door and entered her office, Sister Julian motioned toward the chair at the side of her desk. The weekend had been a particularly busy one with her chairmanship of the regional conference of secondary schools principals, followed by a full day of teaching made necessary by staff sickness. She had been standing in class all morning and now wanted to rest her own feet so invited the girl who had knocked at her study door to sit. Besides, she was intrigued by the fact that this was the Protestant girl who had asked her a question regarding church doctrine a week before.

"Now then," she asked, "what can I do for you?"

"Sister Julian," said Clare, "I've been thinking about what you said last week. About the Blessed Virgin not making a mistake," she added, in case there should be some doubt.

"I remember. Go on."

"In that case, Sister, I think I should become a Catholic."

The Assumption of Mary was winner of the International Writers' Workshop Short Story Competition, 2003 and published in *The Listener,* 15 August 2003.

THE TIDE RISES, THE TIDE FALLS

Cats. They always had cats. Black and white, tabbies, ginger. Moggies, all of them. Her father's term.

Mitzi, her favourite, was grey. A white stripe down the nose. White socks. A good mouser, her mother said. Mitzi or Misty? Mitzi. Definitely Mitzi. When she was sick in bed – measles, chicken pox, one of those things – the cat kept her company. Curled into her. Purring. Kneading with her front paws. Sometime later – months, years, one of those – it was Mitzi who was sick. She'd sit with the cat in her lap. Didn't want to go to school, but they made her. On the second day when she came home Mitzi was gone. Gone to live on a farm they said. A sick cat needs sunlight, grass to run around on. She'd be happy there. Promise? Promise.

After that there was Buster. Large. Ginger. Proud. A ratter. On summer days they'd sit on a branch of the walnut tree. He with eyes closed, purring. She reciting poems learned at school.

The tide rises, the tide falls,
The twilight darkens, the curlew calls;
Along the sea-sands damp and brown,
The traveller hastens toward the town,
*And the tide rises, the tide falls.**

---

*Henry Wadsworth Longfellow: *The Tide Rises, the Tide Falls*

Then Buster got sick. He too went to the farm. A long way away. That's what they said. Another promise.

I want to be a cat nurse, she told them. She didn't know about vets then – there wasn't one in their town. When she was a cat nurse she could cure their pets at home, without them having to go away. That's nice, her mother said.

She became a secretary instead. Thirty words per minute on a Remington Rand Envoy when she started at sixteen. Her first day at Clifford Roberts and Associates she wore a white blouse with Peter Pan collar, and a grey skirt with permanent-press pleats to calf-level. Just an office assistant then, expected to work for three or four years then marry and have a family.

Four years on, fifty-eight words per minute on a Smith-Corona Clipper with speedline body and jet black crinkle paint. Attending night-classes to learn shorthand from Madame LeBrun, later known to be born plain Lillian Brown in Kelburn.

It was from John she learnt to jive and jitterbug. And kiss. No doubt it would have been more had he not been called at short notice to replace another Kayforce volunteer who broke a leg three days before he was to board the frigate in Devonport. When he came back it was clear he was not the same. Gunners never are, her mother said.

By then she'd moved on too. Learned more from Clifford Roberts Junior for whom she took dictation in the late afternoons when other employees were picking up their bags and leaving for the day. Which wasn't enough to stop him from going ahead with marriage to the peaches-and-cream-skinned debutante with prospects assured by a family trust fund.

Her reward, a Royal Quiet DeLuxe machine – with tabulator, paper guide, 'crinkle' finish and chromed bands – as used by

Ian Fleming so a glossy sheet in the carton claimed, though hers was green, not gold. Quieter than the older models she was used to, said Clifford Roberts Junior, repeating and emphasizing the word quiet, pressing his hand on her shoulder, saying he knew he could rely on her. On it she reached eighty words a minute. Under seventy if, while she tapped, she thought about the debutante whose hands remained pale and pristine, unmarred by manual work.

When she thought of leaving, Clifford Roberts Senior persuaded her to stay. By the time the debutante had provided the heir, then twenty-one months later the spare, he had pronounced her indispensable. Who else could he get who used shorthand these days? It was a skill rapidly becoming a thing of the past apparently, though he couldn't understand why. Dictation at one hundred and thirty words per minute, then typing it up at ninety-five on the IBM Selectric Golfball, though understandably fewer if she used the replaceable heads to produce different fonts, italics, and bold characters. As well as the new machine, a new title, office manager, went along with the appreciation.

Ian, the office equipment salesman was keen, dropping in more often than he had new models to demonstrate. The weekend outings he talked her into eventually dwindled as her enthusiasm for movies, beaches, picnics, cycling and even park walks failed to reach the level he judged necessary to consider a more permanent arrangement. By unspoken agreement they both moved on. She to a grey IBM Selectric lll with the new 96 character layout and proportional spacing; Ian to Jeannie, eight years her junior, who she'd trained but whose productivity never exceeded thirty words per minute when errors were factored in.

By the time Ian and Jeannie had produced four children, Clifford Roberts Senior was retired and shorthand skills were not required any more. Her spiral-bound shorthand pad lay unused, behind the stapler and paper punch in the top drawer of her desk. Clifford Roberts Junior had put on weight, his hair thinned till just wisps of grey poked through the pink, and he was not attractive any more.

She was regularly hitting one hundred and five wpm, but her wrists hurt and at night her arms ached up the elbow. When it was increasingly clear from the plethora of typewriter sales in the classified columns that computers were, despite her early prediction, not only here to stay but the future, she made her calculations. Savings accrued from years of abstemious living, if you didn't consider the bin half full of bottles she put at the kerbside every fortnight, a legacy from her parents, and the promise of universal superannuation, would see her right.

Clifford Roberts Junior gave her a dry peck on the cheek as he presented her with the handsome fine china dinner set, and told her she was welcome to take her last machine with her. Both the dinner set and the IBM Wheelwriter, with daisywheel, electronic memory, automatic correction, spell checker and word erase had stayed, untouched, packed in their respective boxes, stored in the wooden chest that sat in the alcove formed by the bay window in her flat.

The chest was the only piece of furniture that went with her when she made her last move. Covered with a damask cloth, it served as a table between the single bed and her armchair where she now sat, massaging her fingers, rubbing her arms, up and down wrists to elbow. Sunlight was what they needed. Yes, sunlight.

If she could find her shoes she'd go to the farm. See

Mitzi. Buster. And the others that came later. She picked up the felt-tipped pen lying on the spiral-bound pad on the damask tablecloth and made some strokes on the lined page. Meaningless strokes they all thought. Sad old dear, they said, she tries to write but can't with those crabbed fingers.

Shoes. She'd need shoes to get there. A pair, black, with heavy soles and low thick heels at the bottom of the cupboard. A grey film over them. Mildew from sitting there for how long had it been, and because that woman who came in to vacuum only ever skimmed over the exposed area and certainly never opened the closet door. Or did they just look grey because of that problem they said she had when she complained about the light being too dim to read by?

Shoes too heavy for running over grass. Mitzi danced in dainty socks.

Someone stopping her as she made her way towards the large doors at the end of the corridor. Taking her arm and turning her around. Calling her Miss P. Remarking on her bare feet. Saying they'd take her back to her room and find her slippers. Sit in your chair and I'll bring you a cup of milk to help you sleep. There you are.

There she was. But she was going somewhere. Wasn't she? Going somewhere. Where? Not to work because her fingers had grown stiff. How had that happened? Not to the dining room. She wasn't hungry. Shoes. Going-out shoes by the open door of the cupboard. The spiral-bound pad with the heavy black strokes on the open page. Horizontal curve with a hook at the end, something a bit like an r, then a hesitant-looking d with a bar at the end.

That was it. She was going to the farm. To find Mitzi. And Buster. But without shoes. In bare feet. So they could run over the grass.

A cup of warm milk in her hand. Someone turning down the covers on a single bed. I was going to the farm, she said. Mitzi's there. And Buster.

That's nice. But it's dark now. Perhaps you can go tomorrow.

Tomorrow. The day returns, but nevermore returns the traveller to the shore. And the tide rises, the tide falls.

Yes. She'd go tomorrow.

LAST NIGHT I DREAMT I WAS KATE SHEPPARD

Last night I dreamt I was Kate Sheppard.

"You should have seen me," I say to Kevin as I sit at the mirror applying my eyeliner, "because I was wearing this amazing outfit. It had an ankle-length dark purple skirt made of the coolest fabric. It looked really classy. Then on top there was this mauve blouse with rows of tiny pin-tucks down the front, and a line of small covered buttons in the middle. And the collar – it was high, right up on my neck, with the most gorgeous mauve lace around it. Honestly, it would cost a fortune at Stax, but I think it would have to be hand washed, or dry-cleaned even, because it looked a bit delicate for the tumble-dryer."

The dryer's my pride and joy at the moment because I've just finished paying it off – fifteen dollars a week out of my wages, which made it a real squeeze what with paying all the rent and the power and the food as well; but gee it's worth it because with working all week I've only got the weekends to get the washing done.

"Oh, and my hair was different too, not short like this. It was long and piled up on my head, the way I'd want it for our wedding. If we ever get married that is. Actually," I add, as he stands by the window towelling his hair dry, "I reckon I looked really nice – like one of those ladies you see in the old photos, you know the brown ones. And, look, if you're going to stand there displaying yourself like that at least pull the nets across." I get up and do it for him because he makes no attempt to do it himself and I don't want that woman over the road stopping me again and complaining when I'm on my way out.

Anyway, in this dream I was at work in my office. I bet the real Kate Sheppard would have got a shock if she could see it, because there we are up on the eighth floor, with floor-to-ceiling glass that gives a view down on the Beehive and the stadium and all over the city; with the telephone speaking to me without my picking it up, the fax machine and the printer both spewing out screeds of paper, and the computer beeping every two minutes to say there's new e-mail.

"And do you know what happened, in my dream?" I ask Kevin when he comes into the kitchen and sits down at the table that I've set ready. I give him his bowl of cereal and he reaches over and takes the toast off my plate, so that as I tell him the story I have to butter and peanut-butter another piece.

"Well, Mr Hamperson came in for his messages and, you know, he's the one I've told you about, that comes right up close and reaches across you so his arm sort of accidentally on purpose brushes your boobs. Yeah, that's right, Sexy Selwyn. Well that's Julie's name for him, but I told her I don't think he's sexy at all, just slimy. Slimy Selwyn I'd call him." I stop to take a bite of toast while I press down the plunger and pour him a cup of coffee.

"Anyway, I was telling you what happened in my dream. Well, he comes in the way he usually does and goes to reach across my desk, as usual. But then he stops and looks at me and it's as though he sees me differently, and well he would, wouldn't he, because I don't normally dress like that, do I? And he sort of steps back a bit, and instead of reaching he asks, 'Are there any messages for me?' and I say, as proper as you like, 'Yes there are, Mr Hamperson', and I hold them out to him. He takes them from my hand without even holding on to it the way he usually does and backs off and goes into his own office. No suggestive sort of questions about how I got on last night, or what I'm doing in the weekend – nothing like that."

"But that's not the best part," I go on. "Hold on Kev, don't go out of the room, because I haven't finished. I'm still getting to the really good bit." So he stands there while I clear the table and put the dishes into the sink and run some hot water over them so I can do them with the dinner dishes tonight.

"Then I dreamt I asked Shirley to make me an appointment with Mr Tyndall, you know, the Head of Human Resources, because I was going to ask him for an increase in pay; and she looked at me as though I was mad and said I didn't have a snowball's chance in hell. But I insisted, and she put me down for eleven o'clock when he had a cancellation."

"So, when the time comes I walk in. That is, I give a tap on his door, open it, go in, and sit down in the chair that the President of Wilson, Madgwick and Saunders has just vacated, and the same one that the Minister of Employment sat in on Friday."

Kevin is standing by the table cutting his fingernails with the clippers and the bits are shooting out in all directions over the floor, so I get the brush and dustpan out of the cupboard and sweep them up while I go on.

"So, I sit there, don't I, and put my case – how I found out that Richard in the accounts section is getting seven thousand dollars a year more than I am and I know that I've been there a year longer than he has. And how I think I should get more anyway now that Stephanie's gone and I've had to take on most of her work as well as doing my own."

Kev starts to walk out of the room without saying anything, so I follow him, still telling him about what happened in my dream.

"Then I see him, Mr Tyndall that is, tap his pencil and look toward the clock. And I've been watching him all the time, haven't I, because of that book on body language I got from the library; and having worked with him for so long I know how he likes to operate. So that's when I hand him the paper I've prepared and brought in with me all ready. It sets out everything I've been saying like a real business proposal – what I'm asking for, the reasons backing it up all lined up with bullet points. And – and this is the clincher – at the bottom I've put a quote."

> *Truer and clearer perceptions of truth and justice,*
> *of rights and duties have been gained... It has been*
> *realized that the peer and the peasant, the male and*
> *the female, are fashioned out of one common clay; that*
> *the accident of birth or the incidence of sex cannot*
> *be allowed to bar the right of each human being to*
> *self-development.*

"And under the quotation I put 'Kate Sheppard, 1919' because I got it out of a book I've been reading about her in my lunchtimes. And then I signed my own name."

In the time I've told Kevin about my dream I've finished making the bed and tidying around. I slip my feet into my blue shoes and pick up the bath towel he's left lying on the bedroom floor and hang it on the towel rail in the bathroom. Then I come back to the dressing table to pick out my blue handbag and transfer my wallet and compact and things into it as I answer his question.

"Kate Sheppard – you must have heard of her. You've seen her picture often enough. Look," and I pull a ten-dollar note out of my wallet. "See," I show it to him. "She was the person who led the women who took on the government ages ago and forced them to pass the law giving women the vote. The franchise," I add, using the word I learned from the book.

Kev takes the note from my hand and stuffs it into his pocket, saying he needs it to buy his lunch. That's going to leave me short, I think, but it'll be all right. I'm meeting Caro at lunch-time. I've been telling her about what I've been reading in the book, so we're going to the National Library to see the original suffrage petition. We're going to look and see if any of our great-grandmothers signed it. Caro will lend me enough for a sandwich till I can pay her back on Thursday.

I begin to tell Kev about handing Mr Tyndall a brochure for the new computer that I'm asking for as well because mine's too slow, but he starts on about isn't it time I got off to work, and to make sure I don't forget to get back in time to run him to his soccer practice. At least he's stopped asking me to lend him my car – he knows I won't while he's still banned from driving. Then he adds that I had better not bloody dream about that woman again tonight because he doesn't bloody want any women with ideas above themselves in bed with him. So I go, but all the way into work I'm thinking about it and, it's silly, but then I find myself wishing that I had one of those blouses that come right up your neck and with all those pin-tucks and lace.

When I get home again after work he's going on about his soccer shorts being dirty, so I start to say, "well you've been here all day," but I can see he's in one of his moods and I leave it. All afternoon I've been thinking that there are some things that really piss me off about Kevin, so I ring up Shorty Allen and ask him to come by on his way to practice and pick him up, so I don't have to wait around down at the park while they play and then have a beer or two.

When the two of them have gone I get down Kev's carry-bag from the top of the cupboard where I put it when he moved in thirteen months and ten days ago and start packing his gear into it. It's big enough, because I don't put in all the stuff I've given him over the past year. I put the bag outside on the front step.

Then I sit down with a cup of coffee and think about all that's happened today – Mr Hamperson with his comments, Kev, and my great-grandmother whose signature I found on the petition.

And I'm thinking that next week I'll look around town for a new top. Mauve coloured, with a high lace collar.

Last Night I Dreamt I Was Kate Sheppard was winner of the Franklin Writers Short Story Competition 2011 and was published in *Breeze 1*, anthology.

Recent decades

The social climate of Aotearoa-New Zealand has changed markedly in recent decades.

Two centuries after settlers from Britain joined Māori as residents of these islands, the country has passed through political stages of colonization, dominion status, independence, to responsible self-government.

Rather than concentrating on its former alignment with Europe, this nation now sees itself as a vital part of Oceania, having strong ties with the islands of Polynesia particularly, as well as Asia, and other countries of the Pacific rim. Increased migration from a wider spread of countries has promoted ethnic and cultural diversity. However, the legacies of this nation's dual ethnic past are very evident, and the country has developed a distinctive culture popularly thought of and referred to as 'Kiwi' after the national bird.

Though not large in geographic size – at 268,021 square kilometres, it is bigger than Great Britain, smaller than Italy, about the size of Colorado – Aotearoa-New Zealand is a full participant in world affairs and has high ranking in social areas such as quality of life, education, health, respect for the natural environment, and sport.

This country's growing film industry has also added greatly to its reputation. The success of The Lord of the Rings *and* The Hobbit *trilogies particularly, as well as many other movies made and filmed here, have added to knowledge of the beauty of this South Pacific land throughout the rest of the world.*

While embracing the technology of the 21st century, Kiwis still remain proud of the 'number 8 wire' tradition that helped create the character of the country and its people. Because of the term's frequent use during the past century, it has come to symbolize the country's citizens – known to be practical, adaptable, innovative, problem-solving people.

THIS BEACH, THAT OTHER BEACH

Her toes dig into the sand and leave scuff marks in the top layer. At this time, on this morning, the sand of this beach is still salt-water drenched, so it is resistant. The day is still early, so it is cool. Soon, when it warms, the fine white sand of this beach will slink through her toes. And it will burn.

Along the empty expanse to her left, is the shelf of rock where fishermen come to cast their lines into the sea. Today, at this hour, there is no one standing on its wave-smoothed top, but it is not because of the warning notice hammered into the foreshore. Later in the day, when the tide is right, people will come. Last season, she knows, three men newly arrived from Asia were washed away from the spot while fishing. A freak wave, one newspaper report called it, but the locals shook their heads.

"More frequent than freak," one said.

The bodies of two of them, broken and lifeless, were recovered. The other was not found.

"They don't know the dangers here," said her brother-in-law.

She expects that he and Sarah are sitting on the verandah of the wooden bach up the slope behind her. Even without turning around to check she is sure they are there. And she knows that at least one of them will stay for as long as she is on the beach. Watching her. Watching out for her.

This beach is different from the other one that fills her mind. On that beach, that other beach, the sand is also fine and white.

It too shimmers in the sun, and in the heat of the day you cannot look at it without dark shades.

But on this beach, at this time, on this day, there are no people. Even at the peak of the afternoon there will be few, compared to that other beach. Maybe there'll be a family with a large umbrella, a rug, and a carry bag of food. Perhaps a person or two on horseback, their mounts leaving a trail of hoof prints as they canter along the high tide line. Or people walking with dogs that sniff the water then take off across the sand to put a seagull to flight before racing back to the water to cool their feet. In the late afternoon a group might arrive, to gather around a portable barbecue or a fire made of driftwood, and sing songs accompanied by the strumming of a guitar into the evening.

Here, unlike that beach, that other beach, there are no lines of sun loungers, constructed of multi-coloured strips of plastic and hired out by the hour, positioned at the top of the sand so their heads are in the shade of the single line of trees that separates the shoreline from the busy town beyond. No carpet of bright towels with bodies clad in sunglasses and brief costumes laid out to be baked by the sun. On this beach there are no hawkers coming by at frequent intervals, with loads hanging from poles across their shoulders as they go from group to group selling canned drinks from a dripping chilly-bin or dishing spicy food onto large leaves from steaming pots. There is no old woman selling sarongs from the array draped over her withered arms – "This the best one for you, madam – this colour go with your beautiful eyes."

This beach where she sits now is backed with dunes lightly spotted with patches of grasses. They stretch for miles to right and left, and only the occasional weathered rooftop appears behind them. Here there is no street where people, overloaded scooters, and cars vie for space day and night. No bars and shops crowded along the far side, so no smells drifting from a hundred exotic dishes being prepared within their walls.

Most of all, here on this beach, there's no Jeff. Not on this day, and now not on any day in the future. Ever.

She doesn't even have a photo of him, of them, in that place – that other place. The pictures are vivid in her mind, they will always be, but there is nothing she can hold in her hand, that she can display to others to show them they were there on that day, that other day. As though people needed to be provided with proof.

She had thought of it that morning, that other morning, when they were sitting on the white sand beach after an early breakfast.

"This is heaven," she'd said, "I want to remember this for ever. We should have brought the camera down with us."

Jeff had grunted and dropped back onto his elbows, his knees raised.

"I'll go back to the hotel and get it," she said, pulling herself up.

"Do you want me to come with you?"

"No, I can go on my own. You stay here and save my space for me."

"Bring my hat when you come back," he'd said, and she'd blown him a kiss as she walked up the sandy slope.

She crossed the street, dodging between trishaws and scooters, and found the alley they'd used as a short cut that morning. It was between a shop selling pirated DVDs and the bar where they'd eaten chicken satay and rice the night before. In the street behind, two young women were entering a property, flower garlands around their necks and carrying trays of fruit. She stopped and looked into the garden to admire a spirit house that stood there, painted white with gold ornamentation on the ornate roofline. It was a pleasing idea to provide a residence for spirits dispossessed from their space when a human habitation was built, and invite them to remain as guardians, protecting the property and its people. She'd take a photograph of that on her way back again when she had the camera.

Across the next street she walked, along half a block passing a building with several unfamiliar flags flying from poles outside, then she turned into the lobby of the hotel. It was tiled and cool. They were lucky to have found one so handy to the beach where they expected to spend a good part of each day they were here. There was no lift. The manager had apologized for its lack when they arrived two nights ago, no doubt having fielded complaints about it before. That was all right, they assured him, even with their room on the third floor. After so many hours on the plane, and with more than a week of leisure stretching ahead of them till after New Year, climbing the stairs would do them good.

Jeff had left the camera on the wardrobe shelf, above the clothes she'd unpacked and hung the day before when they'd finally risen – his cotton shirts draped over light trousers, her skirts and the one long dress brought for evening wear. She reached up and grabbed the strap, pulling his hat down with it and reminding her of his request. It settled sideways on her head, covering one eye. She straightened it and carried the camera to the double doors that opened onto the balcony. When they came back later in the morning she'd take his picture standing there, the blue of the sea showing over the roofs. She wanted a full record of their holiday.

"Why did you take that picture?" he'd asked when she'd snapped one during their long journey south to north. "Airline food is hardly worthy of a permanent reminder." When she switched the display to view mode to reveal his hand resting on the tray table, showing the ring of new gold circling his finger, he'd put a kiss on her forehead.

Her thoughts were interrupted by shouting outside, and a swell of noise. She looked through the glass. Greenery, furniture, and people were being tossed in the wall of churning water that approached. The building shuddered as it hit.

The camera is resting beside her now, on this beach. She picks it up, presses the 'On' button, and looks at the screen showing the three horizontal bands of colour – the white of the sand below, the mid-blue of the sea, and the brighter tone of the sky above. Then she frames the scene letting the rocks, where people who do not understand the danger sometimes stand to fish, intrude on the left border.

The sand feels warmer now on her feet. She knows that soon it will be unbearable, and she will have to retreat up the slope to the safety of the house.

She knows that if you're not careful, this sand, like the sand on that beach – that other beach – will also burn.

THE EMPEROR'S OLD CLOTHES

Clara and Sylvia agreed that Emperor Qin Shi Huang was very superstitious.

"He believed his soul would carry on in another world, so he made sure his tomb was stocked with all the material goods he would need in the next life."

The two young women who conducted the group around the gallery explaining the exhibits were, along with the collected artefacts, also on loan from China. The sleek black bob of the one who made the pronouncement was cut a little longer than the other's – the most convenient way to tell them apart, if one needed to, because they wore identical grey western-style suits with short skirts, red and white pin-striped blouses, and medium-heeled black court-shoes. She introduced herself as Clara and her partner as Sylvia – their English names, of course.

The observation about the Emperor's superstitious nature was inserted into their explanations repeatedly by each speaker as they shared the commentary, each mention accompanied by a slight rising of the eyes and eyebrows. It was similar, thought Tanya, to the look adopted by Craig when he told people "Tanya kisses her Lotto ticket right before they make the draw every Saturday night."

Earlier in the Qin dynasty, explained Clara, hundreds of slaves were buried alive in order to serve the needs of the deceased in their new life in the realm of the ancestors, but this practice was discontinued by later emperors. As she spoke she was dwarfed by two large terracotta figures standing on a raised platform behind her – Qin Shi Huang's replacement for human guardians of his resting place. The expressions on the carved faces no doubt once showed sworn solidarity with their fellows, and determination of purpose. But perhaps the fact of their individualism reflected their creators' satisfaction. Not only did the craftsmen have the fortune to be born in this dynasty rather than a previous time when they themselves would have provided the funerary support for the ruler, but they were also able to gain this measure of their own immortality through duplicating their facial features on such imposing forms.

Now each of the two warriors on display appeared to show pride at being chosen to stand as sentinels over the selected collection of works, even though time had deprived them of their weapons. Now their hands grasped no form of defence, let alone protection. Their separation from their larger army of cohorts seemed to enhance the individual stature of each, rather than diminish it.

The knot of viewers moved on to gather in front of a glass case holding several treasures from the imperial court. According to Sylvia, the ancient people believed in many "fabulous animals". The unicorn – she indicated the figure sculpted of grey clay – was a sacred form employed for protection against evil spirits. Such animals were often carved on tomb reliefs or, like this one, as freestanding pieces. Muscles prominent, legs squared ready for action, head lowered and its substantial horn presented, the unicorn stood at challenge, ready to take on any who sought to affect the desired after-life of the entombed.

It was the two other figures sharing the unicorn's glass case that took Tanya's breath away.

"This is another mythical animal," Sylvia was saying. Tanya slipped in front of a very tall man who was holding a rolled umbrella even though the day outside held no sign of rain.

The deer-like body stood, its four hooves together, on a mount that showed it had once been attached to something else. A ceremonial headdress, Sylvia was suggesting. The creature's head was bowed slightly, both in deference to its owner's status, and in readiness to charge; its pointed ears standing erect and the large curved beak displaying vigilance. Sweeping back over the animal's body was a set of antlers, curving and looping in ornate design, of a size that equalled the body. Tanya looked at the exquisite workmanship of the gleaming gold figure, trying to imagine what manner of person some two and a half thousand years ago would be worthy to wear such a work of artistry and balance.

The rest of the group had moved on to another display where Clara was inviting them to distinguish between three bronze mirrors. Tanya stayed at the case containing the unicorn and the golden creature, her eyes now fixed on its third occupant, a long creeping figure in gilded bronze. The lithe and sinuous shape of the winged tiger, captured so perfectly by its artist, had now held its hunting pose for two millennia. Even in its present sterile setting it evoked images of its former place among peaks and valleys of mystical mountains that lured people with promises of immortality.

Tanya rejoined the other viewers gathered at the collection of oracle bones. She had to look closely to appreciate the depth of skill involved in even the setting out of the translations they bore. Tiny characters written around cracks in cattle scapulae and turtle shells, that in their own time gave advice from heaven, still had the power to bring details of the distant past into the present. In this year of the goat the harvest should begin on the seventh day following the new moon. Should the enemy force known to be approaching from the north arrive before the full moon it would be likely to overcome any opposition that could be raised against it. The illness now raging among the imperial troops was the result of unfilial behaviour in the ranks. Lady Wu was advised to make a major sacrifice at the clan altar – one cattle beast, two sheep, and a dog – to relatives who had passed on recently.

The coffin-like glass case in the centre of the exhibition hall had already attracted half a dozen people as Clara and Sylvia's group approached – independent viewers and returnees from the guided party of the previous hour. Some showed reluctance to move on as Clara led her following to what she announced as the prime exhibit in the collection.

Princess Wan's burial suit, she explained, was made up of more than two thousand pieces of jade. At Clara's urging, Tanya tried to imagine the work that had gone into its making – cutting and shaping of the jade into small tiles, boring holes at each of the edges, then the sewing together with gold thread estimated to weigh seven hundred grams. Thanks to more than a decade of work by the kingdom's top jadesmith, the Princess could rest, assured of her immortality. Clara pronounced the Princess Wan as also superstitious. Sylvia nodded her agreement.

A set of bronze bells, each the size of the glazed tubs into which Tanya had just the day before transplanted the two cabbage trees now placed on each side of the deck off the dining room, proved to be musical instruments. Worked twenty-seven centuries before, each bell was tuned to a different tone, to be played with its companion pieces in ritual ceremonies. Dragons and phoenixes stood in complementary relief, male and female signifying the balance and completeness of the ordered cosmos.

Gold dragons intertwined on the handle of a short sword. The gold, inset with turquoise, revealed its purpose as for presentation at court rather than on the battlefield. Drinking vessels of ornamented ivory, vases and trinkets of translucent jade – all attested to the skills of their artisans who crafted them in a long gone age for use and adornment in banquets and boudoirs.

Tanya moved from the exhibition hall into a small side room of irregular shape, formed from the accommodation of more regular spaces in adjacent parts of the building. The room held a single work on display, though a long form with a blue padded top was placed against a side wall. As Tanya approached the exhibit a man who had been seated rose and left the room. His shoes made no sound on the wooden floor.

The huge vase-shaped vessel was heavy and substantial – a work attesting to the master skills of the bronze forgers of more than twenty-one centuries ago. Eight dragon heads protruded from the most bulbous part near the top of the vessel, with each mouth holding a ball. Positioned on the floor, directly below each of the dragons, with mouths agape ready to receive whichever might fall, sat eight bronze toads.

Tanya read the mounted explanation of the workings and purpose of the world's first seismograph with growing awe. She imagined an official of the imperial court checking each toad in turn and, finding one of the wide grins holding evidence of imbalance in the empire, running to publish an alert – an earthquake has hit in the southwest region. Then the civil defence troops, trained for search and rescue and equipped with supplies, setting out to give aid to the stricken citizens. Such concern for social welfare more than two thousand years ago. It was hard to reconcile with what she understood about the conditions of her own ancestors of the same period.

She sat for some time on the blue-padded bench before she went back into the exhibition hall. Clara and Sylvia, now conducting a new knot of people from the next hour's group, were once more positioned in front of the pair of terracotta warriors. Their slight forms stood in contrast to the formidable figures behind them.

Tanya left the room. As she did so, she could hear Clara telling the assembled viewers that the emperor, and the people of times past, were very superstitious.

The Emperor's Old Clothes was published in *The Listener,* 8 May 2004

HANA, VIGGO AND ME

Hana and Ricky stopped by on their way home. Ricky looked even more relaxed than ever, so I guessed he'd enjoyed himself. Hana was looking rather less at ease.

I didn't have much to report. The kittens' eyes had opened while they were away, there'd been no problems with any of the animals, and as there hadn't been much rain during the week their tank hadn't needed any attention.

"It's still standing," I told them, thankful I didn't have to be the bearer of bad news this time.

"Thanks Jan," said Ricky, "I picked up some new timber and bolts on the way back – that should be enough to do the job. I'll get onto it tomorrow."

He even sounded as though he meant it. I was sure that would bring some comment from Hana, but she seemed preoccupied by something on her mind and it slipped by. That's not unusual when she's returned from down south, and especially when she's been back to Maraekaika for a family do.

"Marae-kai-car," Ricky always refers to it as. "Kai and cars, that sums it up pretty well. When the whānau gets together it's always a competition to see who can bring the most food and who turns up in the biggest car. Talk about competitive!"

"What's wrong with that?" Hana would challenge, "It's better than your lot. We're lucky to get even a cup of tea out of any of the McBrides when we call. They've got the cars all right, but they keep them to themselves. At least our family knows how to share."

"How was the unveiling?" I asked.

"Oh, fine," said Hana and left it at that. It was obvious her mind was still dwelling on something else.

Ricky gave me a look. "It was a good turn-out," he said. "The whānau knows how to support each other – I'll give them that. Cousin Dun even came over from the Chathams."

So that was it. The presence of Dun at any family hui was bound to get Hana's back up. Ever since their teenage years when her cousin had come from the island to the mainland and lived with Hana's family for his secondary school years, the two had been rivals. I'd heard Hana's side of it over many a cup of tea or coffee – about the homework sabotage, the incident over the tree-hut, and especially about how Dun had deliberately worked on winning the allegiance of her dog, Jess, who she'd had from a pup; so much so that when he finally went back home Jess had pined for him and they'd had to send her over to the Chathams. The tears that rolled down Hana's cheeks as she told me of it, some twenty five years after the event, seemed less provoked by sadness at the loss of her pet, than by rage at the memory of the treachery.

I don't know what Hana had done in return. Knowing her, she'd have got her own back, and quite possibly even started it all off, but the feelings hadn't abated over the years. Quite the opposite it seemed, for each time they'd met in the years since then the friction rekindled her resentment.

I'd never met the man, but I knew from Hana's stories that every time Dun flew over from the island to attend a hui at Maraekaika he'd make a point of bringing with him a couple of crates of crayfish, which made him very popular with the rest of the family – a further point of annoyance to Hana who referred to him in mocking tones as "Crayfish Dundee". The fact that the name stuck and was now often used by other members of the family, even if more affectionately, was a source of much satisfaction to Hana.

Usually when Hana and Ricky went over the strait, they drove down to Wellington where they left their vehicle. After crossing on the ferry, they picked up the old Ford they kept at Ricky's sister's in Picton, and which she used to run the children to school on wet days. But when Hana's Koro died a couple of years ago, and she heard Dun was coming over for the funeral, she persuaded Ricky to hire a rental car instead. On the drive south she'd given Ricky strict instructions not to let her cousin know it wasn't their own, and in front of him made frequent references to "our Audi". On the day after the burial, Dun asked Ricky to take him into town for a couple of things, and Hana thought at last she'd made him envious. But during the trip Dun opened the glove box and pulled out the rental papers. For the rest of the week he called her "Avis McBudget", and even introduced Ricky to someone as "my cousin's husband, Ricky Rentadent".

Hana's infuriation was frequently increased by Ricky's slowness or even refusal to back her condemnation of Dun's actions as fully as she would like. Indeed, he seemed at times to relish the encounters and join in the enjoyment his in-laws found watching the one-upmanship between the cousins. He once told me how he and Hana's Koro used to swap yarns about the long-standing tribal feuds between their people and others.

"It's in her blood," Ricky maintained, not only with understanding but, it seemed to me, a certain amount of pride.

Now he laid his hand on Hana's shoulder and turned her toward the door, interrupting her indignation as she told me of Dun's latest offence – wearing a sweatshirt that showed a greatly magnified Chatham Islands group in the central position, with the two major islands of New Zealand much reduced, unnamed, and tucked away off to the left. At the top read the claim: "First to see the light. We lead, the rest of the world follows."

"He was on about it the whole time – couldn't keep his big mouth shut," she said, as Ricky led her through the door.

I didn't hear from Hana for more than a week, then on Saturday morning she called to ask if she could come down for an hour. I had just about finished putting a bucketful of gherkins into jars, and as I screwed down the last cap I heard the trail bike come down the track.

Out of her duffel bag appeared a large sultana cake and an even bigger cabbage. She put the cabbage on the sink-bench, the cake in the middle of the table, took two mugs from the cupboard and put the kettle on to boil. I could see she'd left something in the bag, but knew she'd get around to whatever it was in her own time. We've been neighbours for going on twenty years now – ever since Hana married Ricky and moved up this way. Neighbours and friends.

We carried our mugs into the veranda area I had glassed-in some years ago on the northern side of the house. It's my studio-cum-conservatory, where I often bring my canvases to do the finishing work rather than in the main studio at the back.

While we drank our tea Hana brought me up to date on family happenings – her mother's arthritis, the latest additions to the whānau (one nephew, two nieces), the upgrading of the ablutions block at Maraekaika. Everything except Dun.

Finally, she stopped, and looked around at her bag. Out of

it she pulled a large envelope, and from that she slid a photograph. I knew immediately what it was.

"Remember this?"

I should do, she's shown it to me a dozen times at least.

"I've had a copy made. We need to add some words."

I thought for a moment about the significance of her inclusive pronoun, but from the experience of our many years as friends I knew that Hana was working on a scheme. And I was included in it – like it or not, whatever it was.

Hana's hand was back in her bag. This time it drew out a brown pouch with drawstring and a familiar logo printed in gold. She opened it, almost reverently, and extracted an elegant silver pendant. I'd seen this before too, though not the real thing.

"Is this…?"

"That's it," said Hana. "You see," she pointed to the photo, "he's wearing it in the picture."

I looked. He was. On the chest of Viggo Mortensen, aka Aragorn King of Gondor, lay the Evenstar pendant given to him by Arwen as a symbol of eternal love.

I've learned not to be too surprised at Hana's schemes over the years, but this time I needed a few moments to take it in.

"Where did you get it?"

"Trade Me," she said, "but that's not important."

"It's not the real one?"

"I wish. But I'm going to make him think it is."

I was up with her by this time. I knew she was no longer talking about Viggo, a subject we'd all heard about a thousand times since the two had met when Hana worked with the catering team on the *Lord of the Rings* set. It had to be Dun.

"Your job," continued Hana, "is to go over the writing so it looks like the original."

I fetched a pen and backing sheet, put on my glasses for close work, and under her instruction traced over the words. She examined it critically.

"He'll never know," she pronounced, satisfied.

I thought so too. Even my eye would be hard pressed to tell it from the original that was Hana's pride and joy.

"To Hana, with love, Viggo." She read aloud the words below the picture portraying the two of them – she in her working smock and ugg boots, the Gondor ranger in full costume with his arm around her shoulders.

"Now what?" I asked.

"Now you add some words here." She pointed to the space between the dedication line and the signature.

"In the same writing, you mean?"

"Of course."

The fact that she was asking me to become a forger did not concern Hana a jot.

"Please accept my gift of the Evenstar pendant and wear it for me," she dictated.

"It's too long to fit in," I said, "what about just 'I'll think of you wearing the pendant.'" With my input I was now doubly implicated – but at least the shortened line could be defended.

Hana agreed, and after a couple of practice tries on paper I wrote the words on the photograph. I thought it looked pretty authentic. Hana gazed at it for a full minute, the grin on her face growing more satisfied each second.

I covered the picture with a sheet of tissue and we slipped it back into the envelope. Hana was elated. Barring extraordinary events she'd have to wait a fair while before she saw Dun again, but meanwhile the anticipation was to be savoured.

Hana gunned the motor of the trail bike and shot back up the track spraying dirt and gravel behind. I swear I heard a "yee-ha" as she rounded the first bend.

That night, as my hand passed along the rack of DVDs, it paused at a certain spot. I extracted the disc and installed it in the machine.

"Rest assured, Viggo," I said to myself as I saw the glitter of silver on the bronzed skin, "Evenstar's still working its magic – there's a trick or two left in that pendant yet."

Hana, Viggo and Me gained second place in Franklin Writers short story competition 2013

CROSSING THE BARRIER

From where she was waiting she couldn't see the Boeing touch down, but she knew it had landed. There was a rush of anticipation that rippled right through her, from her throat down through her trunk. He was here. Here, in New Zealand.

She picked up the coffee cup from the table at her side. It was cooler now, but she lifted it to her mouth with care. As she set it down again, the line on the arrivals board clicked to confirm – SQ285 from Singapore, landed.

It was a bare twelve hours since he had called, and she'd heard his voice again.

"Dar-ling." He sounded it the way he did there, in Vietnam, in two separated syllables. The first time he said it was after a full day's surgery in one of the out-clinics. They'd removed the green gowns, changed into their own clothes and headed the jeep back toward the city.

"Another busy day. We're a bit late for dinner, and I could eat a horse." His stomach rumbled as he spoke.

"Then we'll have to stop in town on the way through – there's none of that at the hostel."

He'd laughed. "For all I know it could have been that dish we had a couple of nights ago."

"Have you tried Nuoc-mam?"

"Knock mam – no mam, I can't say I have."

"It's something of a national dish – fish sauce eaten with rice. I know a place where they make it best."

"Laura, once again you're a god-send – lead me to it." He took his eye off the road for a moment as he smiled at her.

At the restaurant he watched as she explained the various dishes.

"You seem so at home here. Especially at the hostel," he added, "when you wear that sarong thing."

"My lavalava – it's not Vietnamese. That's from my time in Samoa. Women here generally cover up more."

"It's really exotic for where I come from. Northumberland's a bit too conservative. And too cold."

"If I were ten years younger, and a few kilos slimmer, I'd buy an áo dài. Like those girls there are wearing." She pointed at a pair of young women cycling past.

"Oh yes! They look so elegant." He repositioned the wooden chopsticks between his fingers. "In white?"

"Why not!"

"With one of those coolie hats to go with it?"

"Of course."

"And ride a bicycle."

"In these streets? You'd have to be mad."

"You seem to fit in so well in this place." He reached across the table and touched her hand. "I think I'll give you a Vietnamese name. Dar Ling. Yes, that's it, Dar Ling."

She laughed as she moved her hand away.

"You don't know the language. It could mean something quite inappropriate."

"Not to me, it won't," he said.

Now, six weeks after she was back home, just when she felt she was re-immersing herself into her old surroundings, letting go of the sights and smells she had come to know over the past two years, she had heard his voice again. Another time she would have been tempted to ignore the telephone when it rang at that hour. Her mother always said that if the phone goes at night after nine o'clock, it was bound to be bad news. Either that or the caller was very inconsiderate. Mother didn't think in terms of international calls – the only time she received one she was woken from her sleep, and would have been relieved to be proved wrong, rather than to hear about the accident so far away.

Last night Laura knew from the first ring it was him. She wrapped a towel around her body, another around her wet hair, and ran into the bedroom.

"Dar Ling."

"Stephen? Where are you? You sound so close."

"Nearer than before. I'm at Changi Airport."

"You're on your way home." The rush of excitement at hearing his voice dropped. Now the distance would widen even further.

Nine thousand three hundred kilometres. The figure had been on her mind each waking hour of every day for the past forty-three days. Now he had come twelve hundred kilometres closer. But that meant he was about to continue his journey in another direction – about thirteen hours to London, then a further flight north till the gap was close to nineteen thousand kilometres. While he was still on this side of the world, a mere five hours behind in the time zones, she could imagine him, working in the surroundings she had come to know so well. Once he'd crossed the halfway marks, in distance and time, he'd be gone, into a world that was unfamiliar to her. But he was talking again.

"Dar Ling – I need to know whether you meant the last thing you said to me."

The last thing.

"Goodbye, Stephen." How could she say more when others were present? If she had trusted her voice to say something further, what would it have been?

It's been good working with you?

If you're ever in New Zealand, do look me up?

It's only another couple of months and you'll be going home too – you'll be back with your wife and family?

But he strode forward, ignoring the right hand she'd given to the other men on the team, and gripped her upper arms as he pressed his lips to each cheek in turn.

"The French do some things best," he said.

The feeling of his touch had remained on both sides of her face for the following hours – in the car, during the flight from Ho Chi Minh City, till she saw the blue of the Straits of Singapore as her plane descended and the first part of the journey that was separating them was over.

The last thing. Goodbye. Was that it?

"You said you wished we could have had more time together, to get to know each other better. Dar Ling, do you still want that?"

So, not quite the last thing. The final words when they were still on their own – that she'd said the day before she'd left, as the truck was turning from the road into the yard in front of the hostel. Words you say when you don't really expect to see a person again.

That night the medical unit, her family away from home, threw a farewell party before her departure the following morning. He'd proposed a toast and started her colleagues in *For She's a Jolly Good Fellow*. Then Katie, the other Kiwi medic in the group, sang *Now Is The Hour* – not really appropriate, she thought at the time, because she wouldn't be returning. Even if she did get home and decide to sign up for another year she would not find them all waiting there when she got back to Vietnam. Most of their terms would be up by then, and they'd be home themselves, wherever that was. Including Stephen. Especially him – his was only a short-term contract and he'd be back on the other side of the world, where he belonged. Under the circumstances, they'd been words that were safe enough to say at the time.

So, what was he asking now? She realized the phone was pressing hard against her ear, and she was holding her breath till he spoke again.

"I can come to New Zealand. There's a plane to Auckland leaving in less than two hours – they're holding a seat for me, but I've got to tell them right away."

She couldn't remember her answer. Perhaps she hadn't given one, but it didn't seem to matter to him.

"That cabin at the beach you spoke about – what did you call it?"

"The bach."

Obviously, he'd remembered that day, just a week before she'd left – the day they went to the eastern coast, a little south of Phan Thiêt Bay.

"How many people are there in this country?" he'd asked as they walked along the sand.

"Eighty million or so."

"That's more than the UK. About a third more – we've got only about sixty million."

"Only! That makes New Zealand's four million look insignificant."

"Four million, is that all? We've got almost twice that many in London."

"Okay – I know when I'm beaten. Why did you want to know, anyway?"

"It's this beach. There's hardly anyone here."

"She laughed. "Look around. I can see houses, vehicles, what about those children, that woman at the water's edge…"

"If this were a beach in England, on a day like this, you wouldn't be able to move for sunbathers and deckchairs."

"Then I'm glad I'm not there."

"So am I, Dar Ling. It's nice – just the two of us, here together."

"You should see some of the beaches we have at home." Her favourite place, the stretch of coastline where she'd spent so many holiday weeks over so many years, was never far from her mind.

"I'd like to." He took a step closer to her. She swung her arms wide to illustrate the scene in her mind, but also to make some distance between them.

"You can be the only person for miles. Our family has a bach at a beach…"

"A what?"

"A bach – a holiday place – where we go for long weekends, and weeks in the holidays. The family's had it for as long as I can remember. My grandfather built it."

"At the seaside?"

"I suppose you'd call it that. It wouldn't be as you imagine it, though."

"Tell me." He reached out to touch her hair. She ducked under his arm and went down the slight slope till foam surrounded her feet.

"There's white sand for miles. When we were kids it seemed to go on forever – we never did walk the length of it. We used to play on it all day – Gary, my brother, and our cousins. At night we'd have bonfires and barbecues. It was our second home."

"A line of houses at a beach?"

"That's the point," she stretched her arms wide again, "There wasn't a line. We were alone. Almost. It used to be about three hundred metres to the next one, and even further in the other direction, but recently there've been a couple more built. Now all of a sudden it seems crowded, but there are still not as many people as there are here. Just a handful, really."

"I'd like to go there. With you." When she didn't respond he reached out his hand. "It's nice – just the two of us. Don't you think?"

"Too nice. I think we'd better go."

She gripped the telephone. He was asking again.

"Dar Ling – can we go to it? To this bach?"

"Yes, if you like." She was still getting to grips with the fact he could be here. It was probably a good idea to have him at the bach – at least till she knew why he was coming. Better than bringing him back to the apartment.

"As soon as I get there?"

"Right away, if that's what you want."

"Great. Can you get everything we'll need?"

"I'll arrange it. When will I see you?"

"The flight arrives at ten-fifty your time. I have to go now and confirm my seat. See you very soon, Dar Ling."

Now he was here. It was still hard to believe. She stood and walked to the escalator, then to the observation area on the third floor. The view from the long window stretched across tarmac and grass to the harbour beyond. The plane was turning in toward the terminal. She watched it make its approach and come to a stop. A train of empty baggage wagons drew up alongside and an air-bridge began to stretch out to close the gap.

She imagined the scene in the main cabin – the succession of clicks as passengers released their lap belts, the way the more impatient travellers already had their belongings in hand impatient to disembark even though asked to remain seated until the plane came to a stop, the opening of overhead lockers and removal of stowed parcels and extra clothing. He'd be in the aisle, bending and stretching the way he did after each journey in the truck between villages. She went back to the escalators.

Downstairs in the arrivals hall a pair of passengers came through the doors that separated the customs-controlled area from the crowd of people gathered to welcome returning friends. The woman was pushing a trolley containing three red and blue striped carrier bags, the contents putting a strain on the top zippers. They'd flown in from one of the Pacific islands, she guessed. A group standing waiting set up a wail and surged forward, surrounding them, and blocking another arriving couple from proceeding further into the hall.

She found a vacant place on the end of one of the groups of seats placed in rows at the left side of the sliding doors and sat watching as the large men and even more ample women took turns to envelop the arrivals in tearful embraces. Several of them placed garlands of crimson and yellow hibiscus flowers around the necks of the arrivals. As the party moved on, two of the men took off their jackets and put them around the shoulders of the pair. She remembered how she shivered for the first weeks she was home.

By now, she estimated, he'd have made the walk through the first halls and would be in the queue waiting to be beckoned forward by the entry officer. If he was at the rear of the main cabin there could be three hundred people ahead of him in the lines – even more if other flights had landed about the same time. There was plenty of time. She stood and walked back to the escalator.

In the first floor store she went straight to the counter.

"The light-coloured jersey on the model at the front – the one with the cable stitch…"

"For yourself, madam?"

"No, a man."

"Size?" She remembered the way her arms had come up at his embrace when they'd been about to get back into the truck after the day at the beach. Before she'd quickly broken free again. He was not as solid as Peter had been, but it was better to be on the safe side.

"Large," she said. She stopped the woman as she reached for a sheet of tissue paper.

"Just a bag will do. And please cut off the tags."

There was a problem with the credit card connection on the first attempt, but she was not concerned. If the lines at the first entry point were not too long it was possible he could now have come down a floor to baggage claim. Even if his luggage was in the first load he still had to pass through the biosecurity check.

A tall man with wispy grey hair now occupied the seat she had vacated in the arrivals hall. He held a spray of miniature orchids. The blooms were smaller, but almost the same vibrant colour as those of the plant that had captivated her during a walk through the city that had been home to her for a year at that time. Her Vietnamese on its own was not up to enquiring about it, but by using the mixture of tongues she usually relied on she had managed.

"L'orchidée la – combien s'il vous plait? Bao nhieu? Cái này tiếng Việt gọi là gì? Quel est son nom?" Good enough to find out all she needed to know about the orchid that had caught her eye. When she left the hostel the care of the *Dendrobium Secundum* was entrusted to Katie, and after her to other successors on the programme. She liked to think of it still there on the sideboard brightening the common room.

She found a space to sit, between a woman holding a toddler, and two jeans-clad young men who sat on the ends of their spines with their legs stretched out in front of them. Both of the boys wore a headset that covered each ear and seemed oblivious to anything around them. They barely moved as she stepped past them. The woman jiggled the child on her knee repeating mantra-like in its ear "Daddy's coming home, Daddy's coming home."

The opaque glass doors slid apart. A woman in a grey suit and black high heels came through towing a single medium-sized case. The three men standing waiting, holding placards with printed names raised their signs to chest height. She nodded at the one on the right. He took the handle of her bag, swung it around, and ushered her through the knot of people standing ready to greet their expected arrivals. Two young men with giant backpacks in place strode into the hall and walked through the waiting crowd without pausing to look at anyone. As they passed she noticed a red maple leaf emblem fixed on each of the packs.

Forty-three, the number came into her head. He'll be number forty-three through the arrivals gate. The businesswoman was one, the two Canadians made three – mot, hai, ba. Forty-three, now what was that? Bon muoi ba. Bon muoi ba minus ba – only forty to go, just bon muoi and it would be him. By now he should be through passport control, perhaps he'd picked his luggage off the conveyor belt and was following the path to the biosecurity checkpoint.

A family of four appeared – mother holding a baby in a pale aqua jump suit and pink slippers, a little boy sitting on top of a suitcase on the trolley while his father held his shoulder – they were bon, nam, sau, and bay. The woman beside her interrupted herself and altered her mantra after the first word. "Daddy's – Daddy's here." She rose, settled the child on her hip, and hurried forward to be clasped by the man who followed the family of four. He was tam.

Why had forty-three come into her mind? It was the number of days since she'd been there – that was it. All those days being neither there nor here, her body in one place but her thoughts still in the other. It would take time, she allowed herself. The country, the people, had got into her psyche. Then just when she felt she was moving on, getting back into the kiwi mindset again, there was the phone call that undid all the progress. And now he was here. Almost.

Two more couples appeared. Chin and muoi, she decided, were just back from their honeymoon – they looked tanned and tired. The elderly pair who were eleven and twelve reminded her of her grandparents. They both had a hand on the bar of the trolley – it turned out of the gate with difficulty.

Muoi ba, and it was him. Already. But it was too soon. She needed more time, she wasn't ready.

He had no luggage other than the familiar working bag he always carried – it was grasped in his left hand, and a plastic carry bag marked "Levi's Changi Airport" hung from the right. She stayed sitting. He was here. In her country – no longer neutral ground. He paused as he looked around, scanning the people gathered waiting. After all the emotion, the preparation, a night sleepless with anticipation, she felt reluctant to move. He walked a few steps further as more arrivals followed him into the hall. Muoi bon, muoi nam …sau …bay …tam – it was only thirteen and he was supposed to be the forty-third. Thirty places too soon, at least.

There it had been a working relationship – the attraction they both felt not acted upon. Now he'd come here what would it be? Just when she was getting back into her life he'd changed the parameters. Though they'd exchanged addresses on that last day there had been no agreement to keep in contact, not even a promise to correspond. And that was the right thing.

For a moment she considered sinking behind the people in front, making her way back across to the door, escaping to the carpark; but she knew what it was like to arrive in a country knowing no one – to experience a measure of reassurance to see her name on a card even though the person holding it was not familiar. Clasping the bag holding the jersey in front of her she stood and walked past the woman in a blue tracksuit and trainers who had just settled into the chair left vacant by the mother and child. The relief on his features when he saw her was clear, and she felt a brief moment of guilt that her own response had not been immediate.

She had wondered on her drive to the airport how their meeting would be. It was unlikely she would know anyone else waiting. Even if she did, all they'd see is her greeting someone they didn't know. There wouldn't have to be introductions. All the same, it would be better to be discreet until his intentions were clear.

Perhaps he'd been thinking the same thing. He switched the plastic bag to the same hand as the other and grasped her shoulder lightly as he leant forward. This time his lips did not touch her cheek – there was no pressure, no feeling of stubble to linger for any time. Just a quick embrace before he pulled away.

"It's so good to see you," he said. "I don't know what I'd have done if I hadn't reached you."

"You too." All the times she'd thought about the possibility of such a reunion her imagination had constructed more active scenes, more confident assurances.

"Here," she said, offering the bag, "I thought you'd find it cold to begin with. I bought you a jersey. It's merino wool."

"Dear Dar Ling – always there to hand me the right thing at the right time. Scalpel, swabs, and now a jersey." He pulled it over his head and thrust his arms through the sleeves. "The right thing indeed. I feel better already. You have a car? Let's go."

"This way." She indicated. "You don't want anything here, before we leave?"

"No. It's better that we get on our way." He stooped to pick up the two bags, then gripped her arm at the elbow and steered her toward the exit sign.

The doors slid apart to allow entry to a group of young women clad in black and gold, holding kiwi mascots. She paused to give way.

"What about your luggage? You must have more than just your day bag."

"That's it. And this," he swung the plastic carry bag forward, "I picked up a pair of jeans and a shirt at Changi."

"You left the rest in a locker in transit?" So, it was just a brief visit. A day, perhaps two, stolen during the journey between two other worlds.

"I'll explain later," he said, increasing his pace.

As they walked through the rows of parked cars they paused to avoid a Subaru Legacy backing out of a space. She recognized the mantra-reciting woman at the wheel. The man who was tam was twisting in his seat, offering a stuffed toy to the child in the car seat in the rear.

Their old roles were reversed, she thought, as she made the turn out of the parking area. Over there it was he who drove. The surgeon before him, the one who headed the team when she joined it, always chose the passenger seat, but when Stephen arrived to fill in between longer-term appointments he'd taken the wheel literally as well.

"It'll take us about fifteen minutes to get to the motorway, then we'll be going southward till we turn off to the east."

"To the bach?"

"It's about a two-hour drive. You doze off if you like. You probably didn't get a lot of sleep last night." She didn't comment about herself.

"Actually, I dropped off right after they served dinner, and woke up for breakfast about an hour and a half before we landed."

"In those seats? I couldn't do it."

"I wasn't in tourist, fortunately."

"You were upgraded? Lucky you."

"Not that fortunate. I paid."

"The New Zealand medical aid programme isn't so affluent."

"Neither is the UK's. It's on my personal credit card."

A maroon SUV ahead of them changed lanes and she eased the pressure on her right foot to allow more room behind it.

"About your bags … you won't be needing much at the bach, but a change or two would have been good."

"The fact is…" he began.

"There'll be a few things there. You can borrow some of Dad's, or my brother's."

"They won't be there, will they?"

"No. Not Dad, and Gary's in England on business. You and he have swapped places."

"Good. I didn't want to see anyone else."

"Yes, that's what I thought." Even though the relationship between them had been a professional one only, meeting others could have been embarrassing for her too.

But there was something he was keeping back. She kept her eyes on the route and the traffic. Four men in lycra, their helmeted heads lowered, pedalled in single file at the left of the lane. After checking in the rear-view mirror, she pulled out to give them space. He cleared his throat.

"I left in a hurry. I went straight from somewhere in the country to the airport. I didn't go back to the hostel, didn't pack up. I've got no luggage – it's still all there." It was clear he wasn't finding the explanation easy, so she gave him time.

"This is the motorway. We'll be on it for a while, then we turn off and go to the coast." She made the turn and merged with the traffic.

"What day is it?" he asked.

"Sunday. You've gained a few hours but not a full day. You're sure you don't want to rest?"

"I was in business class – the seats convert into a bed." All the same, he put his head back on the headrest and it was several minutes before he spoke again.

"Saturday was my day off. I didn't want to hang around the hostel. There was a spare vehicle, so I went for a drive on my own – out of the city."

"Just for a change?" she laughed.

"It wasn't one of our normal routes. I thought I'd just explore, then find my way back, but I made a couple of turns too many and ended up not knowing where I was."

"You needed me there to navigate."

"That's just what was I thinking, when I came to a group of houses. I stopped to see if I could work it out from the map."

"Something happened? What was it?" She checked the side mirror. A car was coming up in the right hand lane – she'd wait till it passed.

"A dog was lying outside one of the houses. It didn't bark."

That was it? The car swished past. She tapped down on the indicator switch ready to move over.

"There was no one in sight. Nothing moving. You know what the place is like – there's always something moving. Dogs everywhere, fowls scratching around."

"What are you saying?"

"They were all dead."

"You went and looked?"

"I went into the houses – each one. They were all dead. Fowls, animals – and people." The meaning of the words was underlined by his tone.

"Bird flu? That would mean it's crossed the species barrier."

"It looks like it."

"There's been no warning reach here yet," she said, "at least nothing made public. What happened when you informed them there?"

"I drove off in what I thought was the right direction. Eventually I found myself near the airport. I stopped, on the spur of the moment. I had my passport in my bum bag, so there was no need to go back to the hostel. I found there was a flight going to Singapore and bought a ticket."

"You left, right then? You found cases of avian flu and didn't tell anyone?" She cancelled the indicator.

"All I could think about was the fact that my term is up in

just a few weeks. If they closed the borders I couldn't get out. I couldn't get back home."

But he wasn't home. He was here, with her.

"Why aren't you on your way to England?" As she asked, she knew the answer. It was a while before he replied.

"It was the shock. I was on the plane to Singapore – I didn't know what to do. I'd left the country, but I didn't dare go home. Just in case. When I got to Changi I looked at the departures board and saw there was a flight out to Auckland. I thought of you."

They were past the succession of off-ramps and climbing the rise. She fought the feeling of repulsion growing inside her, forced her voice to remain calm.

"How long had the people been dead?"

"Not long. When I stopped I went to the first house. The door was open – there was a woman lying on the floor. She had a weak pulse. I lifted her, and she died in my arms. Up to that point I didn't realize anything was wrong. I went to the other houses and found more bodies. That's when I realized the dog was dead. I looked around and found more animals. There wasn't a chicken alive."

The car reached the top of the hill and started down the slope. She had to know.

"But you came here. Didn't you want to see your wife, your children?"

"Of course I wanted them. But, Dar Ling, I needed you."

At the next exit she could turn the car and retrace the course taken so far. She could pull up outside 'Departures' and leave him there.

"What do you think the incubation period will be?" she asked.

"It depends on several factors. Anything between three and ten days. I needed you, Dar Ling," he repeated.

The silence between them stretched. A minute. Another. Three days – and he'd already used one of them getting here. If she took him back to the airport… She flicked the indicator stalk upward and took the left lane.

"Is this the way to the coast?"

"Yes," she replied, "it's about an hour and a half from here to the bach. See if you can sleep." She didn't know what to say, and that would give her time to think.

Ninety minutes later she pulled up at the side of the front deck. He stretched as he got out, in the way she'd seen many times before. He looked well – there'd been no coughing, though it was too early for that anyway. She opened the boot and he lifted out the boxes, placing them on the steps. There was plenty of food for them both for a week. Twice that time for just one of them.

"Leave that bag in the car," she said as he reached for her case. "Here's the key. Can you open up?"

He mounted the steps and walked to the sliding doors. She slid back into the driver's seat, fastened her seat belt and selected reverse.

"I'll phone you each day," she called out, then swung the car out onto the road. As she started the journey back he was still standing on the deck, the key in his hand, staring after her.

DEAR SIR OR MADAM

The District Manager
Work and Income

Dear Sir or Madam,

Subject – refusal to reinstate cancelled unemployment benefit
of Mr Axis Solar

I am writing to request a formal administrative review of the
decision made by one of your officers to cancel the unemployment benefit I have received for the past four years. I have
been informed by the officer in question, and had confirmed
by another officer in the same branch, that in order to have my
application reconsidered I must supply you with further details
to substantiate my credentials. This is in addition to filling in
the usual forms which, I assure you, I have completed on more
than one occasion previously.

The first time was three months ago today when I lodged
my claim at the Ponsonby office. The time was 10.55 a.m. I
can be positive of that even though the day did feature some
stratocumulus.

As instructed, I attended my interview armed with the
relevant documents, viz. two forms of identification (birth
certificate and recent power bill), a bank statement showing
my account number, my Inland Revenue number, a statement

of income over the past 13 weeks (nil), and a statement of my assets that might generate income (also nil).

In addition, and most importantly, on that occasion I produced my updated curriculum vitae with details of my qualifications and work history. This includes a letter of recommendation from my most recent employer, Mr P. Morgan of Eazy Chairs Limited, which clearly states my aptitude for the work I have been seeking recently. I take the liberty of quoting the key passage –

"Mr Skiver is the most dedicated clock-watcher I have had the privilege to employ and I have not a shadow of doubt he will excel in any position that demands this skill as a major part of the job."

It is on the strength of this recommendation that I recorded my occupation as Skiagraphist on my application form.

Before I proceed with an account of my history with your department, it will be beneficial to my case and to your understanding if I clarify certain points.

1. The Mr Skiver referred to by Mr Morgan (letter of recommendation from Eazy Chairs Limited) is none other than me, the undersigned. On taking up my new profession I changed my name by statutory declaration. This was done on the advice of a friend with marketing experience. See documents in the enclosed folder:
     - copy of certificate of change of name,
     - business card for Axis Solar (my new name), of Auckland Sundial Services (my company).

   I believe that the change of name proves my seriousness to pursue my new profession in that:

(i) I sought the advice of such a consultant,

(ii) I was willing to go to the trouble and expense of relinquishing my birth name in order to make it a success.

I declare unequivocally that the move to change my name was in no way an attempt to defraud the Department of Work and Income.

2. Following the closure of Eazy Chairs Limited four years and five months ago I was granted an unemployment benefit, which I received until four months ago at the time of the annual review. At this time I was informed that, due to my failure to actively seek a job (disputed, see below) my benefit would be cancelled.

3. In the meantime, I have used what remains of the redundancy payment received at the closure of Eazy Chairs Limited to cover living expenses, hence the nil balance relating to my assets.

4. In the same period, I have put the time to good effect by studying my new profession and have now been awarded a tertiary qualification. The certificate acknowledging my Diploma of Sundial Studies is at present in the post from Clampett College, Missouri, U.S.A., and I will send you a copy on its arrival. I point out that, since your staff turned me down as ineligible for Training Incentive Allowance funding, I have achieved this qualification at no cost to the New Zealand taxpayer, having paid the fees with the bulk of the redundancy payment. I would be obliged if you could have these fees refunded to me at the same time as the reinstatement of my benefit, or at your earliest convenience.

5. Skiagraphy, being the science of telling time by means of

a sundial, is not to be confused with the art of depicting or projecting shadows as in the practice of X ray imagery. This is a misconception that we professionals in the field do encounter from time to time.

6. Conventional timepieces can be inaccurate as they default to one national time, whereas a sundial is superior in that it displays the time at the exact position of the instrument.

7. There is a distressing lack of sundials in this city.

8. I fulfil all the criteria for receiving the Unemployment Benefit, being a permanent resident over 18 years old, available for and looking for full time work.

The history of my application for reinstatement of the cancelled benefit follows.

On the occasion of my interview with Mrs Condor at the Ponsonby office I supplied evidence of my efforts to gain employment in the area of my expertise. These include –

A. Distribution of my business card (Axis Solar, Dip.Sun. Stud, Auckland Sundial Services) in letterboxes in my area of residence. See the sample stapled to the attached sheet.

B. An advertisement in the trade section of the classifieds in *Sunday News*. See the photocopy on the attached sheet.

C. Phone calls to various sections of Auckland City Council offering my services to advise, install and service sundials throughout the wider city area.

D. Three conversations on Talkback ZB.

Despite these initiatives there have been no offers of employment forthcoming. This is the basis of my application for reinstatement of the benefit until such time as this situation changes. I should point out that at the time of the lodging of my application, I was given to believe that it would be successful and that I would again be receiving the benefit shortly thereafter.

I understand that under the provisions of the Future Focus legislation, beneficiaries can be directed to specific job vacancies, and can assure you that the claim that I failed to attend a scheduled job interview is due to a misunderstanding on the part of the Work and Income office referred to above. For what it is worth, here are the details once again.

Subsequent to my application I was instructed to attend at Auckland Hospital where, I was led to believe, there was a vacancy in my area of work. Imagine the delight I felt at this possibility. When I arrived, however, I was directed to the radiography department, and during the scheduled interview it transpired that Mrs Condor, or one of her colleagues, had fallen into the error of confusing two distinct sciences – see point 5 above.

At a subsequent interview with Work and Income, Ponsonby Branch, I attempted to elaborate on this matter by means of diagrams I had prepared on display cards for the purpose of assisting the department to avoid similar mistakes in the future. I am disappointed to say I found the staff concerned were disinclined to listen.

I assure you that I have since made a full apology to Mrs Condor for the remark I made in the heat of the moment on that occasion. The certificates on the wall of her office prove she is not uneducated and, as I assured her at the time and again since, I have always held the bovine species in high regard.

As to the other matter, that too resulted from an error in interpretation, as I have also tried to explain. My reference, in the presence of the same lady, to lunar cycles was regrettably misinterpreted by her. Should she wish, I will attempt to give her a full explanation of the differences between solar and lunar measurement of time. In fact, I am at present engaged in plans to manufacture an alternative timepiece which will be, in effect, a moon dial and I would be very pleased to show her the prototype.

Given time, I am confident that I, and my chosen work, will make a marked contribution to Auckland City particularly, and to New Zealand society more generally. I am working on several initiatives –

i.   the installation of technology-free time-telling devices throughout the city, a situation that should have a flow-on effect throughout the country,

ii.   the provision of regular servicing of the instruments, including their half-yearly recalibration relating to daylight saving time,

iii.   the reduction of reliance on batteries that are most commonly disposed of in an environmentally polluting way in landfills,

iv.   the formation of an Auckland Sundial Society, which will fill a gap for what has been a neglected portion of the horological fraternity,

v.   arranging an international conference of professional skiagraphists and enthusiasts, which will bring in overseas tourism dollars I estimate to be only slightly less in value than that gained by the Rugby World Cup.

I am sure that you will appreciate the particular appropriateness of these measures, in view of the fact that our country is the one that leads the world in the matter of time.

In the light of these facts and explanations, I hope you will see your way clear to reinstating the Benefit. I am sure you will agree it would be a shame if I am forced, through lack of means, to remove myself to another place taking my skills with me.

Meanwhile, should your department or you personally require any services related to sundials, I will be most happy to oblige.

Yours respectfully,

Axis Solar
Auckland Sundial Services (A.S.S.)

P.S. You will be interested to know that sundial tradition includes that Skiagraphists (aka Dialists) often include a motto on their creations – frequently humorous witticisms on the theme of time. Should your department decide to install a sundial at any of its offices, I have prepared a suitable epigram –

You too are a shadow so seize the day
Both work and income will pass away.

Dear Sir or Madam was winner of the Christine Cole Catley Short Story Award 2013.

THE CALIBRE OF NUMBER EIGHT WIRE

Dave sometimes told a joke about himself. He'd look at a person deadpan and say,

"Some people think I know bugger nothing."

Just as they were wondering how to respond to that, and with timing that would make any stand-up comedian proud, he'd follow it up with,

"But they're wrong. I know bugger all!"

Then he'd laugh, and anyone who didn't know him well would be left wondering.

Not many people got to know Dave well. Even people who had never laid eyes on him, and that was the majority in the district, dismissed him without a further thought, no doubt because of rumours put about decades before. Mostly, when they made their assessments of his faculties they settled for a position somewhere on the downhill side of the IQ scale, covering the range of mental impairment from the harmless oaf to the seriously thick. Not the full quid, the scone dough isn't properly mixed, a stubby short of a six-pack, two kūmara short of a hāngi, couldn't see the road to the dunny if it had red flags on it – all those phrases were repeated time and time again. Plus a few dozen more, and none of them complimentary. The best you could say about it was that the remarks were not made particularly viciously either. No one took Dave seriously enough to put the boot in properly because they didn't question the prevailing opinion about his lack of intellect, and for that reason he wasn't worth the effort.

It wasn't till you lived with him for some time that you came to a different opinion.

It took me a while I have to admit but, like everyone else, I was set up to believe the opposite. When I took on the job of farm manager the implication that Dave wasn't up to much in the brains department was at the very basis of the proposition.

As Lester Forster, the lawyer for the Muldon family, explained the first time I met him in his suite of offices overlooking Garden Place in Hamilton, old Mr Muldon had left the farm property in trust to be run by a manager. His grandson, Dave, was not to inherit, but the terms of the will made it clear he was to have a home at Killin Hills for the rest of his life. Like it or not, the rest of the family could not contest the provision; it was non-negotiable.

The condition that the position, and the house with it, came with an existing resident threw me a bit at the start. Was I to be nursemaid to some kid? I was just a young man of twenty-six myself, and I wasn't looking to take on any extra obligations, particularly to do with children. Young animals were no problem, especially lambs and calves. Piglets and chickens would be okay too – I hadn't had too much to do with them up till then, but I reckoned even those wouldn't pose much challenge in small numbers. The job description had the place down as a medium-sized property being run mainly as a fattening unit with a small dairy herd – just what I was looking for. With the skills I'd built up over the preceding few years it was right up my alley. For my first charge position it seemed a good start, but one thing I was sure of, I wasn't taking on any human livestock. Especially juvenile.

No, Mr Forster reassured me, that wasn't the case. Dave

Muldon was twenty years older than I was. Whoa, another red flag went up. So why wasn't he running the place himself? He wasn't an invalid, was he? I knew to be wary of anything like that too. At the last place I was on – the Haldson property up the Otawa Valley – the manager was always complaining about being hamstrung by the owner. He could feel bloody sorry for the man, he hastened to explain to anyone to whom he was unburdening himself, because sure as hell he wouldn't be very great company either if he was stuck in that chair permanently with a bagful of pee hanging off the side; but it didn't make his job any easier when his every decision about the running of the farm was questioned and challenged.

I was reassured on that count too. I'd have full control. Lester Forster didn't seem inclined to explain any further, so I had to press him. Given the fact it was an odd situation I needed a bit more to go on before I signed any contract.

"You tell me the property belongs to this fellow, Dave Muldon – okay, it belongs to the Muldon family, but he's the only one living there. He's been there all his life, yet you need a manager. What's the story?"

There wasn't much more forthcoming. Mr Forster repeated what was set down in old Mr Muldon's will – Dave would have a home there for as long as he lived but, though it seemed he was a very competent worker on the farm and could carry out the daily chores, there was always to be a manager to run the place.

It seemed, then, the old man couldn't have had much faith in his grandson, so it looked like I'd be taking on a liability. Mr Forster paused, then cleared his throat before confirming my observation, but followed it up with what seemed to be a well-contemplated opinion – he wasn't sure the judgement was deserved. He'd met Dave on a couple of occasions when he'd visited the property and got the impression that though he'd had only basic schooling the man seemed competent enough. But, it wasn't up to the lawyer to say anything, he finished up, I'd be living with him, so I could come to my own conclusion.

So, that was another thing I had to consider. It seemed the accommodation mentioned in the application details for the position – "three-bedroom house, recently renovated, good furnishings and all appliances" – came with a boarder. To be more correct, since it was the Muldon homestead and it had been Dave's home all his life, I was the one who would be the boarder. The further line, "suit first time single manager or married couple without family", now made a little more sense.

The whole proposal needed a bit of thinking about. Mr Forster assured me he understood this and repeated his opinion my credentials and references made him confident I'd make a good job of the position and he'd be obliged if I'd get back to him with an answer as soon as I could – by Friday if possible. Still attempting to find some sort of guarantee, I asked would he mind if I had a word with the present manager, just to check on a few details? Forster looked regretful – he was sorry, he couldn't put me onto the previous manager because the man had left at short notice due to a family tragedy in Australia, and he didn't have a forwarding address at this time. Meanwhile, the day-to-day running of the farm was in the care of this Dave fellow, so it seemed he couldn't be too useless.

A trip out to Tauratahi showed me Killin Hills was a very tidy property. Though I halted at the cattle-stop at the beginning of the agapanthus-lined drive and didn't go on down, all that I could see looked as though it was in good condition. Buildings, fences, and the state of the pastures – the whole place seemed quite prosperous, far from the rundown image I'd anticipated given my conclusions based on the condition in the will.

Over the evening I thought it through. I was more than ready to move on from my current job – I had been for some time. This was what I'd been waiting for, my opportunity for a full manager's position, and it wasn't as though I had a list of other offers to compare it with. Whether having this bloke, Dave, as the unhired help was going to prove the asset Mr Forster suggested, I'd have to see. At least, I told myself, he'd know his way around the place till I was up to speed. As for sharing a house with him, I figured I'd had to bunk in much worse places with an odd assortment of fellow workers over the years, so as long as he was half-way decent I guess I could give it a go. If I could manage to stick it out for a year I'd have the all-important first charge position behind me and I could move on.

As it turned out, by the end of the first year I found I wasn't of a mind to go anywhere.

A couple of months into the job the district Agricultural & Pastoral show came up. By then Dave and I were getting along fine together, as far as I could tell. He'd proved himself more than adequate as a farm worker. What's more, I was pleased to find his cooking left me very satisfied. He seemed happy to take on the task of getting the tucker as well as everything else he did, so I didn't feel I had to take a turn too often.

Another thing I'd learned about him was he didn't drive. In truth, that's not quite accurate. On the property – with farm bikes, the tractor, the ute, over paddocks, up and down hills, across any navigable bit of terrain – he was as mobile as anyone else. I'd even say skilled. The fact was he hadn't ever got a driver's licence and had never sat behind a steering wheel on any road beyond the gate to Killin Hills. If not actively discouraged, I guessed he was never encouraged or given the opportunity. Without a licence Dave was virtually penned on the property. This didn't seem to be an issue with him. Of all the people I've ever met, he's the one who appeared to be the most contented with his life.

When I first mentioned going to the A & P show, Dave took it for granted I would be off for the day. It wasn't a problem, he assured me – he'd be there to do everything necessary. It took a little more discussion for him to realize my intention – I was suggesting we both go. The look on his face led me to ask if he didn't enjoy agricultural shows. Didn't he like seeing the events, and the trade exhibits? Some of our equipment was out of date and was going to need replacing soon – wouldn't he like to check out what was available before we made a decision?

I'd come to the conclusion over the weeks we'd spent together by then that Dave was about the most even-tempered man I'd ever met – his manner didn't seem to vary too far from an equable and agreeable acceptance of whatever was suggested. Now, though, a series of different expressions crossed his face. If I interpreted them correctly they moved from disbelief, though amazement to excitement. It seemed he'd never been to such an event before. Not only had he not attended a show or a field day, it turned out, but even the inside of any of the farm supplies stores in town was unknown territory to him.

Furthermore, the thought that anyone would seek his opinion on any proposed purchase seemed to be beyond his scope. In the past, it seemed, the usual occurrence was that an item of equipment would arrive, and he'd pick up the required skills by watching it being used. With this revelation it was time for me to be out of my depth. Perhaps there was something I was missing. Despite how things seemed here on the land, maybe I was over-estimating Dave in some way. If that were the case, I expected this trip to the show might bring it to light.

The exhibit in the first marquee we visited was promoting a new design in high performance multi-stage submersible pumps that would take a heavy-duty dairy wash down system. After some discussion between the salesman and me, during which Dave stood by listening, the agent agreed they'd come out and give a free demonstration.

"Killin Hills," he repeated as he made a note on his clipboard, "you'll be the new manager then. How are you getting along with that off-sider of yours? I hear he's as silly as a two-bob watch." I took the clipboard and pen from his hand and crossed out the note he'd made.

"We've changed our mind," I said. "Mr Muldon and I will take a look at what the other firms have to offer."

It wasn't the only occasion during the day we came across something similar. Few people in the area had actually met Dave in person, I came to realize as no one recognized him, but it seemed everyone knew him by reputation, even if it was one undeserved. When I tried to avoid unwanted comments by introducing us both at the beginning of any conversation, the curious looks cast in Dave's direction and the deliberate avoidance of talking to him and addressing all the discussion to me, was almost as embarrassing. For me, at least. Dave didn't seem to be nearly as concerned.

He probably picked up on the fact I was upset on his behalf – I was pretty quiet on the way back home, trying to work out just what was going on. We were a few miles out from Tauratahi when there was an explosive chuckle from the passenger seat and Dave came out with his joke.

"Some people think I know bugger nothing..."

I laughed with him, and for the rest of the journey we discussed the various merits of different brands of travelling irrigators, bale feeders, and a proposal for an automated slurry-spreading scheme.

Apart from that one joke, Dave didn't use bad language. Of all the farm workers I've dealt with over all the years, he was just about on his own in that. What's more, I never heard him say anything against another person. I wondered if it was just because he didn't have any real contact with many others, but somehow I doubted it.

After the first time, the two of us often went together on all manner of errands. When I realized how little Dave had seen of even the local area I started taking him along whenever I went out – on trips to town for supplies, visits to neighbours and the occasional stock sale, which he enjoyed most of all. As people got used to seeing him around at different events the odd looks decreased, though what was said behind our backs I can only imagine.

The truth is, if I was expanding his world, Dave was instrumental in shaping mine too. Over the months, which extended into a second year and then another, I found myself settled, happy to stay on in the job, content to spend more time on the property. Contrary to my fears of having to be a nursemaid, I learned a lot from my companion who turned out to be efficient in every task I saw him turn his hand to, either in the house or on the land. Being brought up with farm bikes, I'd never had much to do with horses, so when Dave set about trimming the hooves of the two elderly mares on the property, then reshoeing them, I could only stand by and watch, and admire the way he kept the animals calm as he worked.

Perhaps because he'd been pretty much confined to Killin

Hills for all those years, Dave had a way of finding a solution to all manner of things – making do, with just the materials on hand. At the beginning I'd thought, given his reputation, I'd have to be careful about letting him loose with equipment such as post-rammers and wire-strainers, but it was through observing his skill at fencing that first made me wonder, and question the common assumption about him. Dave could set out with a trailer-load of posts and few rolls of wire and pretty soon there'd be a new fence as neat and sturdy as any I'd seen then or since. The first time I watched him do an end tie-off in about half the time it took me, I stepped up to examine it, thinking there was no way it would hold. With its tight wraps and neat snap-offs, it was superior to my usual effort. It was from him I learned all sorts of tricks including the figure 8 knot. Rather than being mundane utilities the way mine were, Dave's fences were works of art. He could take a roll of wire and make it sing.

In the evenings after we'd cleared away the dinner dishes and I'd entered the day's activities in the farm journal, I'd sometimes get out my leather-working tools and spread them out on the kitchen table. Dave often sat and watched me work. One night, when I was stamping a pattern on a belt I thought I might give him, I asked him when his birthday was. He looked at me in surprise, as though it was an odd question, and after a pause said he thought it might be in November.

"This is November," I said, "what day were you born?" He looked unsure, so I prompted him further.

"Surely you must know. Okay then, are there some papers that can tell you?"

Dave fetched a cardboard box from his room and pushed it across the table. I wasn't sure I should look through whatever was inside, but he said to open it. Whoever kept the family records had sorted them into groups and I found his birth certificate with a bundle of others.

"David Muldon," I read. "Don't you have a middle name?"

"No, just David, I think."

"Is, was your mother Elaine Muldon?" He'd once told me he didn't remember his mother, and that his grandparents had brought him up.

"Elaine Victoria Muldon," said Dave. "Victoria was my grandmother's name too."

I took note of the birth date recorded and resolved to have the belt ready for the end of the following week. In the space for father appeared just the word "unknown". I didn't ask anything more and didn't comment on the age beside his mother's name. I thought of my younger sister who was sixteen, still a kid at school. I refolded the document and replaced it in the box.

"Elaine," I said, "it's a nice name."

Dave picked out a photograph that just fitted into the box. It looked as though it had once been in a frame.

"She's in this picture," he said.

He pointed to each of the Muldon family in turn, identifying them. His grandparents sat on upright chairs, surrounded by their children. Elaine was the smallest one, a little girl holding on to Victoria's skirt.

"What happened here?" I asked, pointing to the left-hand side of the photo, that lacked the white border present on the other three sides. "It looks as though someone's been cut out."

Dave shrugged.

"I don't know. Gran said I shouldn't ask," he said.

I put away my tools and the two of us sat down in the sitting room, as Dave referred to it. The late news on television showed pictures of a whale stranding on one of the east coast beaches.

Volunteers were pouring buckets of water over the backs of the animals and covering them with sacks to keep them wet. I looked over at Dave. There were tears in his eyes and he made no attempt to brush them away.

"Have you ever seen a whale?" I asked him.

"No. I've never been to the sea."

I kept waking and thinking about that throughout night, and the following morning after we'd put the dairy cows through the shed I said to him, "Let's go." We got into the ute and took off.

Several of the pod were already dead when we got there, but a good dozen were being tended by a score or more of people. Some of the workers looked as though they'd been at it all night. One man had an old tractor in the water and was digging out sand on the seaward side of the animals. A couple of boats stood ready to nudge the creatures seaward when the tide reached its peak.

Dave got stuck in helping, and I was reminded of a time a few weeks before when a cow got her head between two strands of fence wire and couldn't get it back out. I'd put my foot on the lower wire pushing it down while Dave pulled up on the other. The old girl should have been able to twist her head and pull it free, but she was panicking by this time and pulling back to no avail. Dave pulled his cutters from his belt and snipped through the strand holding her down, letting her free. Any other farmer I've ever known would have cursed the beast for causing extra work.

"I hope she's okay," was all he said, watching the running cow. He fetched a roll of wire and got on with the repair.

On our way home, back over the Kaimai range later in the afternoon, neither of us was saying much, but I guess we were both pretty satisfied because most of the whales we'd worked with were back out at sea. Then Dave turned to me with a grin,

"It's the first time I've seen the sea. I guess people are right. I know bugger nothing."

"No, Dave," I said, "you're the one that's right. I reckon you know bugger all."

A WHITE HORSE GALLOPED

The first nurse who comes into the room, a junior judging by the lack of lines on her face and epaulettes on her shoulders, seems willing to engage, person to person. She pulls up the chair and sits down so she's on a level with me, the woman in the bed beside her, and making the name badge on her breast with just the word 'Sarah' at the same height as my eyes. Or perhaps she has sore feet from spending the previous night dancing in a disco bar. Good for her, if she did.

She pulls a pen from her pocket and proceeds to work down a list of printed questions, recording my answers on the multi-paged form.

"No," to histories of diabetes, heart disease, hepatitis, HIV, hypertension. The list goes on. In an effort to avoid the tedious I try to vary my responses.

"Negative."

"That's a 'no' too."

"I've managed to avoid that one so far."

With all my answers recorded, she shuts the folder, returns the pen to her pocket and pushes back the chair.

"Don't worry. You'll have no trouble," she says, resting her free hand on my arm. "I hope I'm in as good shape as you are when I'm your age."

"I've lived a pure life," I answer, returning her smile, but as I say the words I find myself wondering – has my life been particularly blessed, or has it been so featureless?

As she goes out the door I look at her retreating back and think, "Go for it, girl. Pluck some rosebuds, put a foot forward and take the step of faith. Launch yourself from the platform in your mind. Take a plane to places you dream about. Ride a horse the length of the Inca Road – Chachapoyas, Machu Picchu, Cuzco, Titicaca." I want to urge her to dance with the revellers paying homage to the Virgin in Oruro, or to the Goddess at a thesmophoria on a warm Mediterranean night. To take a block of stone and craft it into a shape that pleases her, and to keep it in a lush colour-filled garden to remind her that she is fecund, and of what she can create.

I hear the squeak of her rubber soles on polished flooring as she makes her way down the corridor, and want to ring the bell and call her back so I can ask, "Are these your dreams, or are they my regrets?"

The second nurse, the one who comes a half-hour later to insert the cannula into my hand, appears at the door with no warning. She carries a stainless-steel bowl that she places on the locker a little behind my head, out of sight. She pushes the chair out of the way with her leg and stands over me. Perhaps there is a name badge on her uniform too but if so it is high above, at a difficult angle on the top slope of her breasts. My glasses are put away, their arms folded beneath concave lenses in the locker drawer, so to my sight she appears almost featureless.

"I've come to insert your intravenous line," she says as she lifts my hand and inspects my veins, palpating the most prominent one with her index finger. She looks practised, confident. That is reassuring. I consider, and immediately reject, asking her to make a better job of it than the technician on a former occasion, whose efforts resulted in a matched pair of haematoma hillocks before he retreated, shaken, to summon more experienced hands. This one, though, doesn't look as if she would appreciate what might be construed as questioning her ability, and she is the one wielding the needle, so I remain mute.

I avert my head and fix my eyes on the window. When I looked earlier the patch of colour above the top of the white stone building opposite was mid-blue. I remembered likening the shade to the patches of myosotis in the border under the kitchen window. I thought of Emily, her right hand scratching at the skin on her left arm where it disappeared under the plaster cast.

"I can't say that, Nana," she was saying.

"Myosotis," I repeated, "or you can call them forget-me-not."

"Forget-me-not. Forget me not," she recited, plucking a tiny bloom and handing it to me. I bent down and kissed her forehead.

"I won't," I promised, "never, never, as long as I live," and we both laughed.

Now the stretch of blue beyond the window frame has faded a little. It seems to have taken on a grey tinge. I think to myself, when I'm fit again it will be time to tidy that border. Perhaps a complete change is due. It's time to clean out the tired and straggly growth, and replant. I think of night-scented stock, dianthus, and iceland poppies for a winter show.

There is a sharp stinging in my hand. I pull it back toward me.

"Hold still." Nurse Two's tone is commanding. She fixes down the needle with tape – it stabs me as she covers it with transparent dressing. As her grasp releases I reclaim my hand and pull it to my chest folding the other one over it. I feel them both shaking and press them together to keep them still and safe. She pours a small amount of water from a jug into the plastic beaker beside it, and hands it to me, together with a tiny paper cup.

"Swallow these," she instructs.

I wash down the two tablets. Any other time I'd question first.

"They'll come for you in about half an hour. Are you quite comfortable?"

My hand still stings, but I nod.

Her soles also squeak as she moves away, but in a deeper tone than those of the younger woman, and once she disappears much beyond the door there is silence.

Silence. I lie still. I have no desire to read. I'd like to eat but I know it is not permitted, and all temptations have been removed to make sure of it.

The bed to my right is still empty, the way it has been since I returned from my shower earlier this morning. The woman in it, in my estimation a little older than I am, was taken away in my absence, so there was no opportunity for me to hold out a hand in her direction as she went, and to wish her good luck. And now there is no chance of her doing the same for me when it is my turn. It would have been little enough – a gesture between two people thrown together by circumstances, likely never to meet again beyond these ivory-painted walls – but perhaps it would have helped her. And me. Either of us.

There is still a hump in the bedclothes in the place directly across from mine. During the long night past, it was the source of much stirring and changing of position, with light whimpers accompanying each. Now, though, the cotton cover doesn't move. If she were awake it would be someone to talk to, to share concerns and look for reassurances, if either of us wants to talk, but I am glad for her sake she has found temporary relief.

The other bed that makes up the complement of the small ward has not been occupied in the day and a half since my arrival. Perhaps when I am back again, and conscious, I'll find it full.

One gone on before me. One otherwise occupied. One yet to arrive.

I am left in my virtual aloneness. To wait. To think. To remember the clichéd advice that so many I know seemed honour-bound to share in preceding days.

"Relax, there's nothing to worry about, you'll be asleep." And not in control, I'd thought as they laughed.

"There's less risk of dying under anaesthetic than in crossing the road." Yet that's something you hear of every day.

Who mentioned dying, anyway? Should I have come more prepared than packing nightgown, toothbrush and reading matter? Had I thought of it before, I could have made some bequests so that, in the eventuality, a handful of chosen people with no such expectations would, in weeks to come, have reason to be filled with surprise, wonderment, pleasure – in that order – by this tangible token that I had thought about them. That I cared enough to think about what article in my possession might be matched to their personality, or interests. And moved, that I believed them to be a fit trustee for this selected thing. Or perhaps it would serve to make them wonder if they had ever expressed an admiration for the item that led to their covetousness being so rewarded.

But what would I bequeath? Nothing particularly significant comes to mind. Perhaps my subconscious is blocking this eventuality, putting forward counter considerations. What if

I live to change my mind? What if the person picked doesn't want the piece I have selected for them, and another does? I put the thoughts away, abdicating from such decision-making. For now, at least, I will leave the choice to those who are left.

It could, I think, my mind slipping into a more restful mood, be my last chance to play a joke on someone. "To Jessica, I leave all the jewellery, diamonds included, that is stored in safe deposit in my bank." I wonder how long they'd look, just in case there is indeed such an unexpected stash, and how long they will ponder about the identity of the untraceable Jessica. It is tempting, but I let it pass. Now I am here, and at this point, it is too late for anything like that anyway.

There is a low buzz of something that could be a cleaning machine working somewhere. Probably down the corridor, the passage along which I'll be wheeled to the elevator in how long left now? Someone must be about, I think, but no one passes by the rectangle that is my portal to the rest of the world.

Perhaps I should be spending my final hour, if there's a chance that is what it is to be, composing, manipulating – or more likely appropriating – some significant last words that can be quoted with wry smiles as friends gather a few days from now. And which might even be included on the folded printed sheet they'll be given to hold as they sit on hard seats in the funeral chapel wondering how soon they can be on their way, and what they'll have for dinner.

Should it be something heroic? "I am just going outside and may be some time." Sacrificing? "I don't mind if my life goes in the service of the nation. If I die today every drop of my blood will invigorate the nation." Stirring thoughts but, alas, not really appropriate.

Something dramatic, then? "Friends applaud, the comedy is

over." Or philosophical? "What is the answer? In that case what is the question?" Cute, even? "Die, my dear Doctor? That's the last thing I shall do!" Thoughtful, solicitous? "Don't let poor Nelly starve."

When it comes down to it, what better than a thought that's to the point, unadorned, down to earth, prosaic? "Why are you weeping? Did you imagine that I was immortal?" Even if I felt inclined to impart words of well-rehearsed spontaneity, there is no one here to hear them. Anyway, I tell myself, appropriating again, last words are for fools who haven't said enough. So, the one-sided debate falls flat.

I turn my head once more to recheck the patch of blue. My sight seems to take its time following, and the blocks of colour beyond the window frame are indistinct. I shift my hand, feeling for the bell, then bring it back again to rest on the other. It doesn't matter. It doesn't matter at all.

For no reason I can think of, a thought intrudes. Someone, years ago, told me – or did I read it, right now I can't be sure but what does it matter, for the important thing is that it comes back to me now – that someone once asked T. S. Eliot the significance of a line in his poem *Journey of the Magi*.

"And an old white horse galloped away in the meadow".

The enquirer appreciated the other references, the allusions, the effect of the changes of tone in the three stanzas. Grasped the realisation of the hard and bitter agony of the birth that was a death, and even understood the mention of the old dispensation, which was missed by most readers. But what, the questioner wanted to know, was implied by the white horse?

It is said, as passed on by my informant, that Eliot replied the horse simply wanted to be in the poem, so it wrote itself in.

It was an explanation that delighted me at the time and, for no reason I can fathom, the memory brings me pleasure again. The old white horse, its immortality assured by the one-line inclusion, was free to gallop away – to another part of the meadow, to a different meadow or valley, wherever.

Why do I think of this now? Surely, if it's poetry that comes to me at this time, as I lie here waiting, it should be something even more inspirational, heroic. Something to counter my fears, irrational though they may be. Verses to raise the spirit, transport the mind to a higher plane.

Tennyson on the internal conflict of the ageing Ulysses, perhaps, as he readies his ship, planning to embark on a further adventure. He, the great Ulysses, is not that strength he knew in past days. Rather, he is made weak by time and fate. But the hero who strove with the gods is not yet willing to rest from his journeys, still yearning to roam with a hungry heart rather than to rust unburnished. Even in his aged state there is still strength of will. Before the armour that was first Achilles' is again passed on, it is not too late to do some work of noble note, to seek a newer world. In this last journey it is his to strive, to seek, to find, and not yet time to yield.

I struggle, through scudding drifts, to recreate the lines but have trouble grasping them. Someone speaks, but those words escape me too. It is as though I am moving – being borne along on some journey. I allow unseen hands to plot the course and take the helm. I feel a shift in the air as the ship on which I am a passenger tacks and moves in another direction.

A ray of clarity pierces the creeping fog – a shaft of light that reaches upward, out of the gathering overcast. I am being lifted, not upward but sideways. Then settled again in another place, adjacent, just as hard but colder.

Someone, a man I think, his features indistinct, comes into

view. He leans down toward me and lifts my hand – the one that is still smarting because of the cannula.

"When I tell you," he is saying, "I want you to count downward for me, starting from ten."

I sense movement on my other side – something large and pale-coloured coming toward me.

Ten white horses, I am thinking. Nine white horses, eight white horses…

I watch them as they come. They can still gallop.

I urge them on. On, across the meadow. On as far as they want to run. I know, despite the fog rolling over me, their need, like mine, is still to be included.

A White Horse Galloped was winner of a NZSA short story competition in 2010

Glossary

āe – yes

aruhe – fern root, a staple food

atua – deity, deities

a'u – variety of Polynesian tree

auē – alas, oh dear

bach – a small holiday house

bum bag – bag carried on belt around the waist; fanny pack

Chathams – Chatham Islands, a group of small islands about 650 kilometres east of New Zealand

hāere mai – come, welcome

Hāere mai ra i te ahuatanga o to tatau aitua – phrase announcing a death

hāngi – earth oven; meal cooked in it

hāpuka – a variety of fish

Hina-o-te-Marama – woman of the moon, goddess

Hinenuitepō/Hine-Nui-Te-Pō – goddess of the underworld

hongi – greeting by pressing of noses

hui – social gathering

jandal – casual footwear, flip-flop, thong

kai – food

kaihana – cousin, cousins

kāinga – village

karaka – tree, the berries of which are poisonous

karanga – ceremonial call

karakia – chant, prayer, service involving this

kawakawa – a variety of tree

kete, kit – carry bag woven of flax or string

kia kaha – be strong

koro – elderly man, term often used for grandfather

kōura – crayfish

kuia – old woman

kūmara – sweet potato

maipi – wooden weapon

Māori – first nation or indigenous people of New Zealand

marae – gathering place for Maori for social occasions

matakite – a seer, second sight

mate – illness, death

me he korokoro tui – lit. like the throat of the tui; a good singing voice

moa – very large flightless bird, native to New Zealand, now extinct

mokopuna – grandchild

ongaonga – *urtica ferox*, New Zealand tree nettle

Pākehā – not Maori, European

pikau – pack or knapsack

pipi – a shellfish

pito – umbilical cord

pohutukawa – tree, which has bright red flowers at the end of the year

Poneke – Wellington

porangi – mad, insane

pōtiki – youngest of a family

puku – stomach

pūhā – native spinach-like green, sow thistle

stubby – a small bottle of beer

tāina – younger siblings

tamariki – children

Tangaroa – god of the sea

tangata whenua – lit. people of the land, Maori, first nation people

tangi – cry, funeral

tāniko – embroidered border of woven craftwork

tapa – fabric made of beaten bark

tapu – sacred, or forbidden

Te Motu Hōu – New Island

Te Motu Tuarua – Second Island

the strait – Cook Strait, that separates New Zealand's North and South islands

tiare – flower in Polynesian islands

tiki – stylized representation of a human form, often worn as a pendant

tohunga – expert, priest

Trade Me – internet auction website in New Zealand

tui – bird

tungane – brother of a girl

tūpuna – ancestors

unveiling – ceremony of unveiling the headstone of a grave, often at an anniversary of a death

vaka, waka – boat

whānau – family

whenua – land; placenta

*Thank you for taking time to read this collection of stories.
If you enjoyed them, please consider sharing your thoughts by
posting a short review on*

*Amazon (www.amazon.com)
Goodreads (www.goodreads.com)
or other review sites*

*You can also tweet about it, and please tell your friends.
Reviews, either printed or word of mouth, are an author's best
friend and much appreciated.*

Bronwyn revels in sunny days and patting cats. And reading, of course.

In a past life, she was an academic – hence the variation in the sorts of works she has written. She has a PhD from Victoria University of Wellington, but it's the writing career that came first, and to which she has returned in recent years.

As well as books, her hundreds of published works include articles, short stories, poetry, and stage-plays. She has won short story and playwriting competitions and earned other awards for her work.

Currently, she spends most of her writing time on fiction. Home is Auckland, New Zealand's stunning City of Sails, though she is rather inclined to wander other places in the world.

You can also meet Bronwyn at

Website – www.flaxroots.com

Blog – www.flaxroots.com/blog

Amazon Author page – www.amazon.com/
Bronwyn-Elsmore/e/B001JSAPRA

Goodreads – www.goodreads.com/author/show/436327

Facebook – www.facebook.com/flaxrootsNZ

Twitter – www.twitter.com/@flaxroots

Backwards Into The Future

Everyone knows you can't go back. Everyone except Mary apparently, because here she is – back in her old hometown. That's because of two women from the past.

One of them is pushing her, the other is holding back, and between the two there's much to be resolved.

The plum tree and the manuka have gone, but a lemon tree thrives. The mystery of the *Marakihau* may never be solved; but if Ana returns, their friendship and some things from the past can be recovered. Can't they?

Readers say about Backwards Into the Future:

"This is a beautiful, gentle book…it's a marvellous delving into country-town New Zealand in the 1960s… The cross-cultural friendship is also written beautifully…"

"The story is warm and loving and largely happy although there is sadness and tragedy too. I loved the optimistic note on which the book ended."

"It's evocative, gives me goosebumps, compelling and gentle. I loved it."

"Like Bronwyn Elsmore's earlier novel Every Five Minutes, this one is written with a sure, skilled, and sensitive hand. Elsmore knows when to show the finest details, when to drop hints, and when to leave open spaces that readers are compelled to navigate on their own. The story is told gently but never sentimentally. I was pulled into it immediately and it didn't release me until I'd read the last page. I recommend it highly."

Further reviews can be seen on Amazon and Goodreads.

Every Five Minutes

"We are proud to announce that EVERY FIVE MINUTES by Bronwyn Elsmore is a B.R.A.G. Medallion Honoree. This tells a reader that this book is well worth their time and money!"

Book Readers Appreciation Group

A woman, a man, a white dog. The woman calls herself Gina, but it may not be her real name. The woman calls the man Mr Chipzenburger – definitely not his name. The dog is less complicated and is happy to answer to Electra. Their story will make you laugh and cry.

Readers say about Every Five Minutes:

"Bronwyn Elsmore has crafted a beautiful story in a unique way."

"A very unique read to be sure, but her writing brilliance showed on each page."

"A five star read! I hated the story to end. Read it and you'll see. It's a lovely, lovely book."

"A masterpiece! To find that it is perfect in its style and delivery has left me a little breathless."

"This is a love story, NOT a romance, and it's beautiful."

"Thank you for the opportunity to read this wonderful story! I love, love your book!"

"A feel good read. A joy not to be missed."

"It's an ingenuous way to tell the story, and it's exciting to discover a whole new approach to writing."

Further reviews can be seen on Amazon and Goodreads.

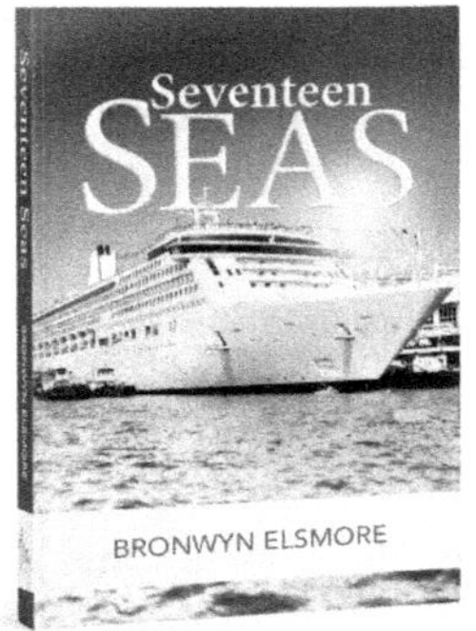

Seventeen Seas

Is there really a stowaway in one of the lifeboats? And what's the truth about Germans and deckchairs? On a cruise ship full of passengers from a variety of countries there's bound to be plenty of fun. *Seventeen Seas* tells their stories through ten countries, fifteen ports, across seventeen seas.

Fiction, non-fiction, humour – *Seventeen Seas* is all of these. The Author likes to describe it as a travel book with a difference. For all who have taken a cruise, think they'd like to, or are certain they never would!

Readers say about Seventeen Seas:

"…everyone will see portrayed someone they know or have met. A great travel book."

"I have recommended the book both to my friends who cruise as well as people who have never cruised and would like to. This book gives a realistic view of what cruising is like in a fun and fictionalized manner."

"I enjoyed the wry humor of this book. And while the subject matter seems light, there is a depth in the characterization and a hidden seriousness that gives the text more depth, and makes it a more fulfilling read."

"The descriptions of different experiences in the ports, their ambience and what they offer make it both factual and informative, as well as engaging equally to those who have been there, and those who would like to visit the ports in future."

"It's the total cruise experience, including sea time activities to port visits, tours, and tourist traps. Having read Seventeen Seas, I feel as though I took the cruise and enjoyed it from my comfy reading chair."

Further reviews can be seen on Amazon and Goodreads.